Critics praise

"A funny, poignant coming-of-age story. . . . Lynch proves himself adept at writing broad, physical comedy, and there's plenty of scathing sarcasm, irreverence, self-deprecation and dark humor to keep things lively. . . . The dialogue is smooth and sassy and crackles with realism."

(starred review)—*Booklist*

"Sports action both hilarious and horrifying (sometimes at once), a slightly larger-than-life cast, and penetrating observations of adults and young adults." —*Kirkus Reviews*

"[A] biting, sometimes hilarious novel. . . [with] plenty of sports action, complex characterization, and a realistic look at growing up male." —*The Horn Book*

"Wise, thought-provoking, and strong-hearted."
—*Publishers Weekly*

Other Books by Chris Lynch

SHADOW BOXER

ICEMAN

GYPSY DAVEY

The BLUE-EYED SON Trilogy

#1 MICK

#2 BLOOD RELATIONS

#3 DOG EAT DOG

CHRIS LYNCH
SLOT MACHINE

HarperTrophy®
An Imprint of HarperCollins Publishers

Slot Machine
Copyright © 1995 by Chris Lynch
All rights reserved. No part of this book may be used or reproduced in
any manner whatsoever without written permission except in the case of
brief quotations embodied in critical articles and reviews. Printed in the
United States of America. For information address HarperCollins
Children's Books, a division of HarperCollins Publishers, 1350 Avenue of
the Americas, New York, NY 10019.

Library of Congress Cataloging-in-Publication Data
Lynch, Chris.
    Slot machine / Chris Lynch
        p.   cm.
    Summary: When overweight thirteen-year-old Elvin Bishop is sent to
camp at Christian Brothers Academy Retreat Center, he and his two best
friends are forced to try various sports in order to find out where they
belong.
    ISBN 0-06-447140-3 (pbk.)
    [1. Camps—Fiction.   2. Sports—Fiction.   3. Identity—Fiction.
4. Friendship—Fiction.]   I. Title
PZ7.L979739S1   1995   94-48235
[Fic]—dc20   CIP
                                                                 AC

Typography by Al Cetta

❖

First Harper Trophy edition, 1996

To Mikie Hunt, wherever the hell you are

PART I
WEEK ONE

Chapter 1

A fine how-do-you-do.

How many friends do you need?

Two. You need two friends.

There's the big circle of people you know, some of whom you like and some of whom you don't, which is fine. Then there's the tighter circle inside of that, with the people you like a little more and also including the ones you dislike a little more, which is also okay. Then at the core there are the real ones, the friends who wind up meaning everything to you in the end, and this is tough, being so close, but worth it, and if you've got more than two you probably have too many.

Two was what I had. That's what I wanted, and I wasn't looking for anything more. I figured I was better off than most people, having two good friends.

I even had them arranged. Mikie was Friend One.

Mikie was the guy who had begun to look like me because we had spent so much time together. Even if he was thin and fair-haired and I was not. Even if no one could see it but me. Mikie was the guy who *knew* me. Mikie was the guy who could say things to me.

We were on our way to The Camp. "Please, Elvin, please, stop reading the stupid brochure already," Mikie said, snatching the glossy "Twenty-One Nights with the Knights" camp booklet out of my hands. Then he grabbed my neck, twisted my head so I was looking out the window at the evergreens whizzing by. "We're on the *bus*, Elvin. We're *going*, understand? It's not like you're still making up your mind."

I didn't fight him. I sighed. I stared. Fine, let him steal my brochure, I already had it memorized anyway:

Q: Who are we?

A: We are the Knights, the flagship Christian Brothers Academy of the entire East Coast, representing the highest ideals and achievements of disciplined Catholic education.

Q: What is Twenty-One Nights with the Knights?

A: It is a leg up, a jump start, a fine how-do-you-do. It is a three-week camp for incoming freshmen, designed to ease their transition from junior high to the fast-paced world of high school, from young men to men. It is an introduction to the Knight Ethos, in which our students are welcomed into a tradition of excellence in education, spirituality, and athletics. It is where our students join our family. After attending Twenty-One Nights with the Knights, your first day at school in September will be not a journey into the unknown, but a homecoming.

Q: What will we do during our twenty-one nights?

A: You will have fun. We insist. We've designed a program of swimming, hiking, baseball, tennis . . . you name it. Invigorating. Thought-provoking. All in the idyllic rolling green hills of the St. Paul's Seminary Retreat Center. You will meet new friends you'll keep for the rest of your life. You'll have such a good time, you won't even realize how much you've learned and how much you've grown until it's all over. And when it is over, you'll wind up feeling—as most of our men tell us—that Twenty-One Nights are just not enough.

"Twenty-one nights, Mikie," I blurted, having kept quiet for as long as I was able. "Nobody's supposed to do any one thing for that long. Couldn't they just have a party or take us all to a Red Sox game if they wanted to get us together?"

"Here," Mikie said, sticking the brochure back in my hand. "I'd rather have you reading the thing than talking about it anymore."

Mikie was not concerned. He thought the camp idea wasn't so bad. "Come on, El, what would we be doing anyway? Sitting around staring at each other all through July like we did last summer and the eight summers before that. Frankly, and don't get all pissed

5

off now, you get a little boring after about the second week."

I got all pissed off.

"You'll get over it," he said, shrugging.

I popped a cookie and covered the rest of the package with my forearm. My mother had packed me an entire package of Nutter Butter cookies for the bus trip. Because I'm fat. Not hugely fat, like I'm about to have a baby, but moderately fat, like I just had one two or three months ago. The fat was a problem, but this was her way of saying the fat was yesterday's problem, and maybe tomorrow's, but the antisocialism was today's problem, and if she had to toss a couple of barbecued chickens onto the bus and slam the door behind me, she'd do it. So I had the cookies. With Mikie being useless, the cookies helped.

"You sharing?" Frankie asked.

"I'm not," I said calmly.

"Then I'm stealing, huh?" he said as he took a cookie anyway.

Frankie was Friend One-A. Frankie was the kind of person who was just too beautiful to be anybody's Friend One. He could have a personality like Mister Rogers—which anyway is about the opposite of the personality he does have—and still the long curly auburn hair, the puffy heart-shaped mouth, the gray patch that said he could have a mustache if he felt like it, the Bermuda-water green-blue eyes and the way-too-manly shape of his body, would always work against him. The thing that was different about my One and One-A friends was that the first was kind of low-key cool and cautious and the second made you feel like you were doing something wrong just to be with him. The thing that was the same about them was that they both did and said absolutely whatever they wanted to me.

Frankie reached over from the seat behind me, pushed my hand aside, and grabbed four more cookies.

"Listen to this, Elvin," Frankie said with *my* cookie rolling out of his mouth. "You just don't see this the right way. Look at it as an adventure, as a new experience, instead of the same old thing. While you're sitting there mooning over the stuff you did when you were a *kid*, there's a whole new world slipping away."

"You sound like my mother," I grumbled.

"Well, she's right," Mikie kicked in.

I spiked a Nutter Butter into my mouth, then talked with crumbs shooting. "No, no, you guys don't get it," I said. "You're the *kids*, remember? This is how it's supposed to go: I tell you what a heartless beast my mother is, and—here's the important part—whether I'm *right or not*, you're supposed to say, 'God, Elvin, raw deal. Parents suck.'"

Mike turned away from me; Frankie snatched another cookie from over my shoulder and sat back to enjoy it.

"It ain't a kids' camp anyway, it's a *men's* camp," Frankie roared as the bus made a noisy lunge up a small hill. I turned halfway around in my seat so I could see both of them at once. "It's all about man stuff, strictly for those of us who are, or *aspire* to be"—he wiggled his eyebrows up and down at me—"men. I think it's a great idea. A *huge* idea. Like, the best idea ever. They're going to make a *man* out of you, Elvin."

"Right. That's what they said in every prison movie and every war movie I ever saw."

Mikie stood up. He put his hands on his hips and stared back and forth at me and Frankie, like a teacher. "Open the windows. Get yourselves some air, will you, guys? *You*"—he pointed at me—"think we're going to Vietnam. *You*"—he pointed at Frankie—"think we're going to Fantasy Island. I think we're going to *camp*, like a million other guys, ya dopes."

Mikie dropped into his seat, and we all stayed quiet for a few seconds.

"I don't like it," I said slowly.

"I love it," Frank said.

Mikie sighed, and joined me as I pored over the camp brochure.

"That looks nice," he said hopefully, pointing at a color photo of a bunch of boys playing a smiling game of volleyball next to a barbecue.

I was seeing something very different from what he was seeing.

"'A COMMITMENT to excellence' . . . 'The ideal setting to buffer the pain of transition for our fine young MEN' . . . 'We STRONGLY encourage all our incoming freshmen to attend' . . . 'A BONDING experience they will carry for a LIFETIME . . .' Mikie, do you see this? I mean, what's with all those capital letters? And how about that 'pain of transition' deal? All right? They already know it's going to hurt. Am I the only one worried about this?"

"I think you are, El," Mike said.

Frank leaned over me again and stole another Nutter Butter. But he didn't eat it. "Jesus, have a cookie, El." He jammed it in my mouth and sat back.

Suddenly, the guy in the seat in front of me turned around. He was a box-headed mouth-breather with black eyebrows as wide and shiny as a Groucho mustache.

"I thought I smelled peanut-butter cookies," he said, and helped himself. "Thanks."

I looked down into my lap. I heard Mikie chuckle. Then I saw another hand in my Nutter Butters. I looked up to see Box-head's seatmate. "Thanks," he said, grinning.

I could feel myself turning red.

"They're just screwing with you, Elvin," Mikie said. "Don't let them get to you."

Frankie scooted up behind me and whispered in my ear. "You want me to stop him, El? You just say, and I'll take care of it."

I shook my head, waved him off.

"Yo, anybody want some Nutter Butters up there?" Boxy yelled. When everybody on the bus called back Yes, he turned to me again, reaching.

I covered up the package with my hands. "You know, maybe if you asked . . ." I said weakly. "If you just asked . . ."

"Oh, pretty please," the Box laughed.

"That's enough," Mikie said. "Leave him alone."

The guy arched those unbelievable eyebrows at Mikie, then stood. He had to bend his beefy neck to keep his head from bumping the curved ceiling of the bus. "So, whatchu gonna do about it?" he asked.

Before Mikie could say anything, Boxy's eyes moved to beyond us, where Frankie was standing. They stared at each other. "You wanna die, boy?" Box-head said.

"*Maybe* I'll die," Frank said, "but for *sure* you won't be having another one of his cookies."

I looked up toward the front of the bus, where the monitor was. He was looking at the situation but pretending not to.

"All right, sit down now," Mikie said when things hung there all frozen. "This is stupid."

"Shut up," Box said.

"Hey, Elvin," Frank said coolly, "think I could have another cookie?" I could hear the grin, even though I was no longer looking at him.

I passed the package back up over my head to Frankie. He took the whole thing; then I heard him sit down with it.

Box now looked even dumber. He was standing alone. I didn't have the cookies. They were in the seat behind me, and if he wanted to get them, he had to be serious about going after Frank. Slowly, awkwardly, he slid back into his seat.

As I listened to Frank munching happily behind me, I buried my face back in the brochure.

The only thing we GUARANTEE is that you will carry this experience with you for the rest of your life.

Elvin Bishop
Route 95 North
Seat 38

Elvin's Mother
Home Where Elvin Ought To Be
USA

Ma,

Retreat. That's what they call this. Did you know that? It's not a camp, it's a retreat. They didn't exactly define it, so I looked it up in the dictionary. They may mean definition 3, "a place of seclusion or privacy," or definition 4, "a period of retirement for meditation." But since they've left it open, I'm going with definition 7, "to slope backward." I'm comfortable with that.

I'm blossoming already here. Made new friends before I even got off the bus. The cookies were a great icebreaker.

How are those crab puffs, Ma? Puffy enough? Crabby enough? I feel so guilty gorging myself on these luscious liverwurst fritters while you suffer through back on the home front. Just say the word and I'll have a bushel sent to you. Go ahead, just say the word. Go ahead. Say it, I said.

Love,
El

"There is no such thing as liverwurst fritters," Frankie said as I lay on my wooden slab of a bed, writing.

"Stop peeking over my shoulder," I said. I folded the letter and stashed it in my locker. "And fine, then you tell me what we just ate."

"Ah . . . calzone."

"No way."

"Corn dogs."

"Corn dogs are shaped like hot dogs. These were shaped like cow pies."

"Uh . . . okay, so what, Elvin, so they were liverwurst fritters. They were fine. You have to stop complaining about everything. We've been here for three hours and you already have a reputation as a whiner."

"Ohhhh," I whined, "now who said thaaaat . . . ?" I flopped back down onto the bed, stretched out, stared at the brown water spot on the ceiling directly above me.

Frank came over and sat on the edge, pushing me. "Scoot over there, will you?" He gave me a series of shoves to make room for himself, as if I had anywhere to go. The big part of me hung over the other side of the bed.

"Listen, El," he said very seriously and quietly, as guys unpacked and wrote letters and burped up liverwurst all around us. "I'll help you out here, but I can't do it all. You have to make some kind of effort. Certain kinds of guys get picked on more than others. Try not to be one of those kind of guys."

"Ya, like fat guys," I said. "What, am I going to not be fat while I'm here?"

"True, the fat doesn't help," said Frankie. "But that's not it. You might as well be wearing a sign that says, 'Hi, I'm Elvin. Abuse me.' I mean, you have to be fat, okay, but you don't have to be a dink or a geek or a feeb or a simp."

"That's just what my mother said when . . ."

"And stop talking about your mother all the time. Toughen up. Grow up. I'll let you in on a little secret here. . . ."

"Don't tell me any secrets, Frank. I don't want to know any secrets. I like not knowing what I don't know."

"It's simple," he preached on. "Act like me. Don't make that face, Elvin. Junior high is dead." He made a loud smacking sound with his big lips. "Kiss it good-bye. Bigger things lie ahead. You can't be a lump anymore—you have to be a *mover*. Like myself, for example."

What he was referring to, of course, was his *style*. He knew that he was pretty and manly at the same time and all grown up before the rest of us, and this gave him confidence. It was only a matter of time before the almost lewd, rock-and-roll way he acted in junior high went from "problem behavior" to star power. Nobody understood that better than Frankie himself.

"God's gift to himself," the girls in the school yard would snap as they sneaked peeks at him from behind.

"Yesss," he would respond, hearing them every time.

But it was dangerous to act like he did. He acted big and beautiful because he was. Some of us were not equipped.

13

"Just try it," he urged, waving me up off the cot, trying to raise me from the social dead. "Trust me, it's all in the way you act. If you act like a slug, you'll be a slug. But if you act like *moi* . . ."

I stood, moderately inspired.

"There you go," he said. "Honestly, *I* act like me all the time, and it still makes me all tingly.

"And besides," he added, "if you act like *you* here, they'll kick your ass."

I lay back down.

"And I won't let them kick your ass, El," he said, resting a hand on my belly. "Sure, I'll die for your cookies, but I'd really rather not. So go ahead now, take a nap. This will work better if you have all your strength."

They gave us an hour after dinner to either barf it up or keep it down. I figured it was one of those trial-by-fire things that would make men out of us. The kind of stuff that happened to Jesus and A Man Called Horse in the movies. I sweated it out on my bed, made it through cold turkey, did not lose the dinner. The first test was passed; I had a hunch it wasn't the last.

Then we had to return to the scene of the crime, to receive The Message.

"We're going to take the measure of you, men" were the first official words we heard. We were back in the woodsy A-frame dining hall/auditorium, and Brother Jackson was talking. He was in charge. In charge of the retreat, and in charge of the school. He wasn't the headmaster; that was just a figurehead job. Jackson was the real thing: *Dean of Men.* I couldn't wait to put that in a letter, because I was sure my mother would think I made it up.

Frankie leaned into me. We were at the core, the nub of the nub of the sweaty gathering of three hundred new freshmen. Frosh, we were called. A forest of half-popped Adam's apples.

"They want to take the measure of *this* man, they better have a yardstick handy," Frank hummed.

He had said so many things like that before dinner on this first day that I hardly even heard him by then. I was scanning the crowd for Mikie.

"Slotting," Jackson boomed, his microphone turned up twenty times louder than it needed to be. "Slotting, we call it. We believe that each man has got a slot, a place in the big scheme of things, and to maximize the potential of each, it is in everybody's best interest to find that slot at the earliest possible time."

"I have a slot," Frankie mumbled, "but *he*'s not going to find it."

"Where's Mikie?" I asked. "You seen him?"

"Ya, he's right over there." Frank waved his arm over half the hall, covering a hundred and fifty or so guys, giving none of his attention to me and all of it to the indoctrination. He actually seemed to like it.

Frankie was fitting in too well here. It was frightening. I needed Mike. Frank needed Mike too. While Frankie was game for anything, and I was game for nothing, Mike was Dad. That's what we called him back at the old school, Dad. Everybody called him that, because of his sense, his radar for always knowing the way to go. Do this one. Don't do that one. Don't go there. That's not funny. That's cool. Everyone joked about it, called him Dad as if it was a cut. Sometimes, when he was too sensible, it got on our nerves. Then we called him Dud.

But we always listened to him, or wished we had. It was just a gift, something that was built into him. He was never wrong. I knew that for a fact, because he told me so.

We got split, though. Me and Frankie in one cabin, Mikie out there somewhere in one of the other nine *Families*. That's what they called each group, a Family. As if we were different species of bugs, or Mafia factions. Whatever they called it, I didn't connect. I felt like a baby bird dumped out of the nest, plummeting. I needed Mike. Frankie was like another baby bird dumped from the nest, but rocketing straight up. He needed Mikie too.

"I want to introduce to you men," Brother Jackson boomed on, "Mr. Buonfiglio, one of our senior instructors here at the retreat. Now some of you may know Mr. Buonfiglio as the coach of our school's Division Two state champion football team. But that's not the reason he's here. That would violate state regulations regarding having organized football camps before August fifteenth . . ." Like a comedian, Jackson let his words trail off as he scanned the audience, a sly smile spreading across his black thread lips. "And we wouldn't want to do *that* now, would we?"

Hearty yucks started bubbling out here and there as guys started getting the joke.

"No, no, no. Mr. Buonfiglio is here in his capacity as freshman history teacher and academic advisor . . ." He didn't have to pause for a laugh this time, the crowd picking right up on it, Buonfiglio blowing hard on his whistle—his academic advising whistle—to big applause.

"And this," Jackson said, putting his hand on the shoulder of a taller, leaner, but just as grim-faced man as the not-football-coach, "is Mr. Rourke, who is *not* just the coach of the *three-time* state championship cross-country team, but also the study-hall proctor and guidance counselor. . . ."

This was apparently the funniest thing anyone there had ever heard. The A-frame rocked under my feet and over my head.

On and on it went, through the murderers' row of coaches who were teachers. I learned something as I shriveled in the middle of it all, hands cupped over my ears. I learned that the easier it is to spell someone's laugh, the stupider that laugh sounds.

HOF-HOF-HOF-HOF was popular close to the stage.

HAR-AR-AR-AR-AR was the choice of most tall guys, the basketball players sprouting up here and there throughout.

GUH-HUH-GUH-HUH-GUH-HUH. God, the guh-huhs, bone chilling in their ignorance, they rose from all corners, like a noxious gas that you couldn't see, but was going to get you.

HEE-AWW-HEE-AWW was Frankie's brand.

I knew that, wherever he was, Mikie wasn't making a sound.

Mother,

Football camp. You sent me to football camp. How sweet. How did you ever guess? I did try soooo hard to keep my passion for smashing into other fat boys a secret, but you found me out, didn't you? Who told? Come on now, who told?

Yours Muy Macho,
Elvin "Big Booty" Bishop

P.S. How do you like my new name? I hope you like it a lot, because apparently it's mine to keep. Locker-room camaraderie stuff, you know. Please address all my mail accordingly from now on.

We finally located Mikie and used one of our precious twenty-minute "Reflective Periods" to go see him. We get Reflectives three times a day: before breakfast, after lunch, after dinner. It was the only officially sanctioned time when we were not accountable to one function, one counsellor, one location or another. Deep-thought time, to pull it all together, sort things out, see ourselves at one with . . . spiritual stuff. To the naked eye, it looked like almost everybody got closer to god in one of three ways: 1. smoking cigarettes, 2. sleeping, or 3. conducting party-of-one religious services in the bathroom.

We found Mikie in Cluster Seven. No, they're not cabins, they're "Clusters." Frankie and I were clustering way over in Number Two.

Mikie came out and sat on a rock, hunched over, his chin on his fist. "I don't know . . ." he kept saying while shaking his head. "I don't know . . ."

"What happens if we escape?" I asked.

"You guys are big babies," Frankie said. "When are you going to grow up? This could be the most fun you ever had. What, you want to spend all summer with Mommy?"

"Yes," I blurted.

"I don't know," Mikie repeated. "It's not so much the camp. Three weeks isn't so hard. I'm just not so sure about the school. Is this what it's going to be like? They're a little . . . gung-ho for me."

"Jeez, that's exactly what you guys *need*," Frankie said, "is a little gung-*ho*." He pumped his fist when he said *ho*. "You're the two boringest guys in the whole camp—"

"Retreat," I corrected him.

"The two boringest guys in the whole retreat. I mean, I'm compromising myself just being seen here in the open with you." He looked all around, as if the geek police were gaining on him.

"You been slotted yet for tomorrow?" I asked Mike. For starters we were allowed to tell the administration what we were best at, and if there was space, that was the area, or "Sector," we'd go with. Then, after checking you out, if they decided otherwise, you'd be slotted elsewhere. So you gave them a list of at least two specialties.

"Hoop Sector," Mike said, shrugging. "But I told them if they wanted I could also do Baseball Sector or run some track. How 'bout you?"

"I abstained," I said.

"That was *so* damn embarrassing," Frankie said. "In front of the whole Family."

Mike liked it. "Abstained?" He laughed.

"Told the counsellor—all right, how's this, his name is *Thor*—that I was a conscientious objector, that the whole slotting thing was degrading, and that I had a lot of unslottable intangibles to contribute to the school."

"Uh-oh. What did he say?"

"He scribbled for like five minutes in his notebook, then said they'd get back to me."

"Yikes," Mike said.

A bell gonged high up in the tower. Reflective Period was over in another five minutes. Time to hurry back to the Cluster to be with the Family.

"So what's your slot, Frankie?" Mike called as we started back up the trail.

Frank spun to face Mikie, walking backward now. "Come on, Dad," Frankie drawled, "what's *always* been my slot?"

Mikie started shaking his head again, pointing sternly as Frank slapped himself on the rear, then galloped away like a horse. "Better watch yourself, Franko," he warned.

What had Frankie's slot always been? *Big persona*, mostly. And he set out immediately to make it so here too. First night we established the routine, everyone in Cluster Two gathering around for the stories. In another camp, they would have been ghost stories. Here, it was Frankie telling amazing-Frankie stories. My job was to nod, to corroborate, to verify that yes, I swear to god he did that, he actually did that. More or less.

"You remember that nun, don't you, Elvin? Sure. She was a novice, actually, not quite a nun yet, still on the fence, *if ya know what I mean*." He grabbed his thigh when he said it, and whenever he said it, he charged that phrase—*if ya know what I mean*—with more secret, smutty meaning than anything that ever popped up in the letters to *Penthouse*. "Well I'll tell ya, she was on that fence when she came to our school, and she was tottering pretty bad when she left. Am I right, Elvin?"

I had forgotten if he was, strictly, right. But he told it so well, told it so *good*, that he always had me believing in him. "You are right, Frankie," I said. I could enjoy this for a while, basking in a little bit of Frankie's raunchy glamour. It was as close to the real thing as I was likely to get anytime soon.

"She wasn't a nun like, you know, nuns. She was young. She wore a pair of Guess? jeans sometimes in the afternoons when she raked the churchyard, and let me tell you, she didn't embarrass herself doing it either. Everybody fell in love the day she showed up, boys *and* girls, no lie. She looked like Keanu Reeves."

21

"Oh, you're full of it, man," one big guy, football slotted, challenged.

Frank just tilted a glance my way, and I did my thing. I raised my hand, put on my Boy Scout face, and said, "I swear. It's the truth. It's all true."

"Thank you," Frank said, bowing graciously.

"No, thank *you*," I replied. I never wanted him to stop.

"Listen, guys," Frank went on, "I don't blame you. Half the time I look at my life and I can hardly believe it myself. But there it is."

"So what happened?" an impatient desperate small voice shot through.

"Well, I just told her, I said, Sis, I'm tight with the Lord, and we got an agreement: I don't steal *his* chicks, and he doesn't throw me into no whales or turn me into salt."

"What did she do? Come on?"

Out of his version of modesty, Frankie gestured to me to finish.

"She killed herself," I said flatly.

They all moaned; somebody booed.

"Well, they transferred her anyway, after she took the pills. And we *heard* that the next time she really did it, with the hair dryer in the bathtub."

"Lights out," the voice called, and the lights snapped immediately off.

"Nnnnnnnaked. And dead. In the bathtub," Frankie hummed like the devil in the darkness.

22

Frankie always told stories to get a reaction. Laughs, applause, and gasps for Frank were like blood for a vampire. So he was probably satisfied, after lights-out, to hear the symphony of rusty bedsprings *eek-eek*ing all over the barracks.

"Pace yourselves, boys," I thought, "or you'll never survive three weeks with the guy."

Mrs. Bishop,

There are no girls here. Ma. None. Not even a nun. Even the big ugly nurse and his assistant are male. Did you know about this? If it were not for Frankie's imagination, we would all be dangerously lonely here. Have we thought this out all the way? Do we think this is a good thing for me at this stage? All right, let it be on your head, Ma.

Fine. Whatever. I'm sorry, I'm being bratty. I shouldn't be raining on *your* summer. How are those World Cup games going anyway? Pretty ripping, huh? Was that you the paper showed sitting in the party tent with Placido Domingo after Italy-Spain in Foxboro? He was looking down your dress, you know. Did I *not* tell you to avoid the European men while I'm away?

No Longer Your Concern,
Mr. Bishop

23

Chapter 2

Oh my god. Football.

What to do with the fat guys? They don't know what to do with the fat guys. The fat guys don't fit the Plan, the Philosophy, the shorts. Red shorts. Everybody's got to wear them. The Plan is that all the fine young men here can succeed if they are properly guided to the right sports activity for them. The raw material is in there, in each and every one of us, and it can be molded with the proper instruction at the earliest levels—before we get too screwed up.

I tried to tell them. I tried earnestly to tell them that my insides were every bit as flabby as my outsides. They wouldn't hear of it. None of the people in charge here—and they were *all* in charge, except for the kids—could conceive of this. They'd call up their directory of everything they knew about young men's insides, and that profile would not show up. The soft kid, the kid who could not play anything and who did not even care about it. They were sorry, but that kid did not exist.

"We'll find what you're hidin' inside there," said Thor, my Cluster Leader. He grabbed two fistfuls of fat at my beltline and yanked me around as he said it, like a hundred people had done before him.

Why do people think that's funny?

Football, of course. Their response to a fat kid is always football. They don't know what else to do. They figure they're going to melt away my outside and find a football-player-shaped monster lurking on the inside.

They just wouldn't listen.

"Don't cry, goddammit," the coach screamed. It was my third play from scrimmage, eight minutes and three head slaps into my football career. "It's a head slap. It's illegal, but it happens all the time. You can't *cry* about it. Jesus." He turned his back on me and stalked away, personally offended by my behavior. Then he paced, as violent people will do when they're trying to get it under control.

I wasn't crying, anyhow. Yes, I was upset, and yes, there were tears splashing down my face, but I was not crying. They were just those pain tears, the kind that come out when your mind says "no way, not now, cannot cry here" but your body knows better and goes ahead unauthorized.

I could feel around me that I was getting looks from the four score and seven other gridiron monkeys who stood in temporary grunt-free silence all over the field. Hell, half of them had cried already, but they channeled their pain in a much more acceptable way: They went on and maimed somebody else.

Composed, Coach came back as I lined up again. He screamed right into the little one-inch earhole on the right side of my helmet, so it sounded like he had a bullhorn pressed to the side of my head. "Do not let him get by you again! Your quarterback was a dead man on that last play! Protect the passer! Don't cry! Don't cry!"

"I was not crying," I yelled, because it seemed pretty important to establish that. It didn't matter; the coach was already back to pacing, walking me off his mind.

The snap, my man rushed me. Pushed me, two hands flat on my chest. *Bam.* Pushed me again, blasting me back a couple more steps. I tried to dig in. Useless. Crowded me. *Clack*, his helmet banged into mine. One punch in the stomach. My wind gone. I was practically running backward. "Jesus Christ," I heard the desperate-sounding quarterback behind me say. I was just trying to fend my man off now with stiff arms, waving hands. *Bang!* Left-side head slap nearly knocked me over until *Bang!* right-side head slap rocked me the other way. My head hit the turf before my hands could brace me. I heard the thud of the quarterback being driven into the ground behind me.

I couldn't get right up. Which was not a problem. Coach came to me.

"Stop crying," he screamed. "Jesus, I hate that." He

lunged at me as he spoke, like he was going to hit me himself.

It didn't bother me much. I had enough on my plate just trying to get up. As I pushed to try and get some space between my throbbing head and the earth, it felt as if I was lifting the planet off of me, rather than vice versa. I paused for a few seconds on all fours, touched my face lightly with my fingertips, and felt the blood drip from my nose. A couple of guys got me by the armpits and brought me to the nurse's station.

Sick bay. Full of slackers like me. Skinny kids and fat kids. Sick bay—or "Injured list" or "IL," as they prefer to call it—is a very hot ticket, especially in the first few days of retreat.

In fact it's so popular that they issue us vouchers for IL time. You get four vouchers, each good for an hour with the nurse, or a half day if he declares you a wreck. Seems that in years past out-of-shape guys were always taking dives and hiding out in sick bay for most of camp. Hence the voucher system. If you ran out of vouchers, you were not allowed to go to the nurse if you could get there under your own power. And if you couldn't, it was a judgment call made by the coach.

I was lying on my cot, a cool ice bag across my sinuses, musing on a way to retroactively flunk my way back into junior high, when the guy in the next cot broke the dream.

"What you in for?"

I opened my eyes, turned slightly to look. "Wow," I

27

said as I took him all in. He was lying on his stomach, stretching out way over both ends of his little cot, even farther than I overlapped the sides of mine. Can't have the tubs and beanpoles getting too comfortable down at the clinic, now, can we?

To the untrained eye, this could have been a player. But one glance and I knew better. I recognized the look.

"Basketball slot, huh?" I said wisely.

He nodded, then winced with the pain of nodding. "Football slot?" he asked in return.

"Ya," I said. "What happened?"

"Undercut. Went up for a rebound and somebody took my legs out from under me, landed right on my back. You?"

"Head slaps. Nosebleeds. Public humiliation." I kept nodding as I talked, he kept nodding as he listened. Like we'd all been here before, more or less.

The nurse's assistant, Butch, came over and stood between our cots. Regaining speech control was the official first sign of readiness to return to the general population. Butch himself barely qualified. "You can get up?" he said to my new geeky friend.

"I not can get up," he grunted slowly.

When I laughed, Butch set himself on me. "You. Bleeding stop?"

I removed the ice pack, brought two fingers to my nostrils.

"Hey. Do that again," Butch insisted.

"What? This?" I asked, and touched my nose again.

28

Butch pulled me up by the wrist. "Hell, if you can do that, you're ready to go back. Stop wastin' my time."

Before I was forced out, I leaned down toward my comrade. "Elvin Bishop," I said, and shook his hand.

"Paul Burman," he said in return. He smiled through real pain. "Cool. I haven't actually made any friends here yet."

I didn't want to lead him on. "Oh, well, see I already have two friends, so I'm all set for now. But . . . well, we'll see." Then I dropped into a whisper for what I was really after. "This for real?" I asked, pointing at his back.

He nodded.

"Good for you, Paul. Listen, you know where a guy can get his hands on a couple of extra vouchers?"

"Nah. But you dig any up, let me know."

I said I would, then felt myself being tugged by the back of my T-shirt. Back *there*. My heart sank.

"I'll see you, Elvin," Paul said, yelling straight down into the floor. "Probably right here, I'll see you." Probably he was right. I returned to the fields.

"No, there's nothing I can do about it. You've *gotta* be a lineman," the coach growled, too disgusted to even scream at me now. "What am I gonna do, make you a flippin' *cornerback*?" He got a lot of laughs with that one. Laughs from assistant coaches. Laughs from jock student football team counsellors. Laughs from kids who were built to be real cornerbacks.

Laughs from lumpy scared fat kids. Who should have been better than that.

That was when I shut up.

I took my slot and I didn't make a sound about it. I played both sides of the ball. It didn't matter a whole lot except that when I was a defensive lineman I didn't get beat so bad. One time I even made a tackle when the running back ran right into me, drilled me with his helmet in my belly.

I fell down. I gasped for breath, every play. I ate wedge-shaped orange pieces and threw the peels on the ground with two thousand other peels. I sweated. My armpits, my chest, my back, the crotch of my too-tight red shorts were all soaked through before anybody else's. But then it all blended together, and my stuff just looked darker. My nose bled two more times, once from a head slap, once when a guy stuck his fingers up through my face mask.

Three o'clock the whistle screeched. I made it. Without a sound, without a tear. Walked off the field just like everybody else. Only last. By a long way.

Mother of all Mothers,

Wish you were here.

I know that all kids write that from camp, but *I* really mean it. I wish you were here with me today, shoulder to shoulder, holding that line. Together, we could have done it. As it was, my success was a little spotty.

I did have a spiritual moment, though. Once when I

30

had a little unscheduled "Reflective Period" at the bottom of a pig pile, I saw a tunnel and a glow and somebody foggy saying, "Come to the light. Come to the light." She looked like you. But that wouldn't be you, Ma, now would it, Ma?

If this is looking a little squiggly, it's because I'm writing with my left hand. Why am I writing with my left hand? Because that's the hand that still has two fingers that can curl. Doesn't look half bad, though, does it? There you go, another hidden skill the camp experience has drawn out of me. I was really dogging it back home, wasn't I? Tomorrow they're going to have me snag a salmon out of the river with my teeth.

Ug,
Elvin, Son of a Bishop

P.S. I'm getting a lot of special attention here from the football coach. I think I'm his favorite. You better watch out or you could lose me. When this is all over, I just might be going home with Knute.

Chapter 3

Oh my god. Still football.

Pain is one thing. Pain is trying to hang a picture of Curly Howard on your bedroom wall and bashing yourself in the head with the rounded end of a ball peen hammer, just like Curly would have done. I've had that. Pain is food poisoning from meat knishes. I've had that. Pain is trying to help out around the house, washing the dishes, and just as your mother says, "Careful of the blades on that food processor . . ." I've had that.

But this. The morning after the first day of football. I had slogged through thirteen pretty rugged years up to this point, yet I had no idea a feeling like this was possible. A picture of my mind would have looked like a rat frantically scurrying around a maze, trying to locate one tiny spot that was not searing hot and shot through with spikes of pain. My joints, my muscles, my skin, my organs, there was not a safe, pain-free spot anywhere, inside or out.

I woke at four thirty. I lay stiff until five. It was peaceful at first, in a near-death sort of way. An owl hooted mellowlike. Then dawn broke, the owl fell asleep, and some mental wild birds started screeching—at me. In my head, the screeches came together and sounded like words, the way the loon's call sounds like "Looooon."

Outta bed. Outta bed, one bird called.

Ouch, the other replied.

Outta bed. Ouch. Outta bed. Ouch. Outta bed. Ouch.

I got out of bed. Ouch. I was aware, way too aware, of being, of being here, of being alive, whatever that amounted to. I couldn't just float through this the way I usually could when I wanted to be where I wasn't. I couldn't pretend, imagine it away, the way I needed to. With every step, every flex, the muscle or joint or bone would scream, reminding me, "*Zing!* You're still here. *Zing!* It's pretty bad. *Zing!* There's plenty more where this came from. Today." I closed my eyes and sniffed up the wood of the old floor and the pine just outside. There was an actual outdoorsy camp feel to the place, retreat or not, that was reachable and pleasant when everybody was asleep. I was almost there. I almost reached it, that better place.

Then my hamstring tightened, then twisted, like something chewing on the muscle, pulling me down into a squat, pulling me back down to earth.

So I was still here. I couldn't get out, not for a minute,

33

couldn't even pretend my way out. More than anything else, this worried me. Because if a guy can't do a little pretending when he needs to, can't take a little trip on the inside—that's when the guy is really truly trapped. Really truly trapped.

"Well then, what *are* you good at?" Coach snapped. He'd just given us our morning pep talk on how much sex and mayhem we would enjoy if we would ever make his glorious varsity football team. Then we broke up into groups for drills according to position—offensive back-field, defensive backfield, receivers, linebackers, and linemen. I told him I was misplaced with the linemen, and that's when he asked me the pointed question of the day. I hesitated a couple of nanoseconds so he asked me again, only louder and funnier for his audience.

"So, Bishop, what the hell *are* you good at?"

What I wanted to say was, "I'm a kid, asshole. Give me a milk shake and a game of Monopoly and I'll *show* you what I'm good at." But I couldn't say that. So I said the opposite.

"I can play quarterback," I said, shocking myself with brilliance and stupidity. Playing the line was just too slow a death. I wanted the express.

Anyone who has ever been inside of a ringing church bell probably can appreciate the sound of ninety hopeful thirteen-year-old football ruffians *yeowww*ing at the same moment. Anyone else couldn't imagine it.

"Quarterback?" Coach asked in mock seriousness when he could talk again.

"Quarterback," I assured him. "I have an arm like a shoulder-mounted missile launcher. But more important, I have the *mind* of a quarterback." I tapped myself on the dented temple of my helmet.

"Oh, gimme a break," the real quarterback said, snatching the ball away from the coach. The three other backup quarterbacks did what backup quarterbacks are supposed to do: They backed him up.

"Gimme a break."

"Ya, gimme a break."

"Gimme a break, wouldja, fat boy."

"No, no, no," laughed the coach. "Bring that pigskin back here. Kid's got some balls he wasn't showin' before. I like that."

Mouths dropped open everywhere when Coach flipped me the ball and called out, "Live drills, live drills. First teams line up over here on field A."

It had gotten serious. Nobody laughed now. I found myself nervously reading players' faces to try and see my immediate future. Grim. The tough players looked tougher. The medium players looked out of it, dumb-founded. Only the marginals, the fourth and fifth and forget-about-it stringers, looked sympathetic. On their faces I saw sympathy winces, practicing for sharing my pain.

"Know any plays?" Coach asked.

"Of course," I said. "I was a lineman yesterday." And surely I did know them. There were only two pass plays, and I had had an intimate look at them over and over as each play unfolded above my prostrate body. So I got to study the whole process, the way fish must watch fishing from beneath a glass-bottomed boat.

I called out Plan B. I swear I heard giggling from my own offensive line as I grunted out meaningless decoy numbers and directions before taking the snap.

"Hut, hut, hut." I'd thought I would never get a chance to say those magical words into some guy's big butt. But here I was. It was a storybook ending.

"Hut, hut, hut."

My hands were sweating so hard, I spent the entire six seconds of my dropback trying to squeeze a grip on the ball, passing it to myself from hand to hand, to knee, to hand. I wasn't even looking up at what was coming my way until finally, just balancing the ball on the fingertips of my throwing hand, I looked up. I shouldn't have.

How true it is that the greatest things in life seem to whiz by a person—like Alfredo sauce in a fantastic northern Italian restaurant—and the most wicked things always take forever to unfold, dragging and dragging and dragging by in almost suspended motion until all the agony has been wrung out of them and into you.

Whether my linemen merely stepped out of the way, or whether the defense was just so hungry to get me that they were unstoppable, I'll never know. All I know is that I raised my eyes just in time to look directly into the face mask of the animal who got there first, and see over his shoulder as the ball flitted off to a better place without me. The guy was just then landing from leaping at me.

The grille of his mask pressed into mine, so I could watch the shifting of his insanely gritted teeth while he carried me down. When we landed, we bounced. He bounced right over me, ripping my helmet along with him. This made way for the second guy, who landed high, his protective cup smashing me in the chin. It was just as hard as a helmet, only somehow more degrading. A third guy drove his helmet into my side. The fourth ambled up casually and just fell on me. I made a sound like a whoopee cushion out of both ends as all the life gasses fled me.

The stretcher I was carried away on was wider and softer than the cot I slept on. The sky was powder blue and blissfully, peacefully cloudless. The stretcher carriers were good, very good—in sync, gently swinging me as they all stepped together, left-right-left-right. I thought, "I might like to ride in a hot-air balloon someday, just like this. Blue."

I was a success. One play, and I was out.

"Making a mockery of my fine football program," Coach was muttering as I wafted by. "*Mocking* it. Mocking *football*?" he questioned, in total disbelief.

"Hut," I said. "This doesn't count, does it? Hut. Hut. If I can't make it on my own? Hut, hut, hut. This doesn't cost me any vouchers, hut, does it?"

When they got me back to the nurse's station, I perked up. I felt like I was home. "Hi, guys," I said to all the people I didn't know. I felt great, but I was still lying down.

There was no available cot for me because apparently

day two is the biggest day for sick bay. That's when all the other athletic bottom feeders wake up and realize what I was sharp enough to pick up on day one. Which is: "Holy shit, Batman, get me out of here."

So they dumped me off the stretcher and propped me in a chair. I no longer felt great. I slumped forward until one of the stretcher bearers put a big paw on my chest and straightened me up. Undaunted, I slumped again. He straightened me again. The nurse came over, joined in a discussion I could not hear clearly other than a few angry "Coach says under *no* circumstances is that kid allowed . . ." and dismissed my assistants.

"How are you?" he said, but he didn't care. So I didn't answer. Then he pulled out a little capsule, broke it open under my nose.

"Yeowww!" I hollered, and snapped my head back. It burned my nostrils, my eyes, and my throat. "That smells like ammonia. Times ten."

The nurse smiled, whipped out his little penlight, and started looking into my eyes as he talked. "You have answered correctly, have passed the examination, and are free to go."

"Go?" I asked. "I didn't even get to lie down and regroup. You're supposed to let me regroup, aren't you?"

"Are you suffering any headaches?"

"No. Not yet anyway, but I'm sure I will. It's a little early to tell yet, don't you think? Maybe we should hold me over for some observation."

"Look," Nurse said, pointing over his shoulder at the

basket cases who had beat me to the cots. "I have a lot of real injuries to treat here. We've got an unusually soft crop this year."

I looked around him at the patients. Holding their knees, holding their elbows, rubbing their heads. And moaning, every one of them. They were good. There was a lot of talent in the room.

"Oh, what?" I pressed. "Because they're moaning? I can do that. *Woooo-ohhhh-ooooo*," I sang, wrapping both arms around my head. "But I didn't want to make a big fuss. I believe a man should suffer silently."

"Good," Nurse said. "Then do it outside." He pulled me up out of the chair by the hand.

When he got me up close, I came clean. In a whisper, however. "Please, please, please, you can't send me back there. I won't make it. I can't do football again. I don't know what that coach guy has planned for me, but I won't survive it. I won't. He's probably X-ing and O-ing out a plan right now in the dirt that ends with me decapitated. Did he ever send a kid home dead before?"

Nurse watched me and listened with wide eyes. "You don't have to worry about all that. You've got special orders *not* to return to the Football Sector."

I jumped up and down as if I had just scored a touchdown, even though my head really did hurt now. I spiked an imaginary football. "Thank you, thank you," I said, pumping Nurse's hand. Then I slowed down, touched my temple gingerly. "You got anything for my head?"

He reached into the pocket of his baggy white pants

and pulled out a few packets of Tylenol. "Here. This is all I can do for you now."

I told him I would get by on that and shuffled happily along, waving to all the poor saps who were going to be sent back to the front no matter how much weeping and wailing they did. I stepped out into the sunlight and sucked it all in. Free. I felt so free. This was an unusual freedom, because normally they only did slotting in full-day increments. Even if you washed out, you finished the day in the slot you were in, then you got reslotted the next morning.

But not me. I was a special case. For almost one whole day, I was a man without a slot.

One giant "Reflective Period" was what I had. I used it to make a tour, to see finally what the hell was going on here. I could do that because of my special status. I was momentarily unattached. And if you didn't belong to a group around here, a mystical thing happened—nobody in that group could see you. You didn't register.

The camp, retreat, compound, the joint, was actually a seminary, set on a few acres of small green hills. A very pretty place surrounded by evergreens. It was easy to see why it would be a good place for the kind of spiritual get-aways they held here the rest of the year. They had only three or four actual seminarians on the premises, and we hardly saw any evidence of them at all. They were mostly just black laundry hanging on the line outside a dormitory.

Whatever it was—seminary, camp, retreat—it was

impressive, and overequipped. They had a white brick gym building the size of Madison Square Garden, complete with a hockey-style hanging scoreboard and retractable bleachers. I pictured it: those long midwinter nights when the seminarians needed this stuff for a good game of hoops, one on one, with a third guy at the scorer's table and the fourth being the crowd. But when I wandered in, there were about forty guys down on the floor and a handful of counsellors in the stands.

I saw my buddy from sick bay, Paul Burman. He wasn't half bad, but still I could see he didn't belong here in Basketball Sector. He was the tallest player by a head, but he only put the ball in the hole when there was no other choice. On most teams a guy like that would be option one—feed it to the big guy. But it was clear the big guy didn't want it. The team would push up the floor, players dig in under the hoop, the pass would come inside, defense would collapse on Paul, and he'd kick it back out.

Then somebody else, a forward, put up a jumper. It missed; Paul grabbed the rebound—soared, two feet above the rest—then passed it back out again. His face remained frozen through it all. He didn't smile. He didn't scowl in intense pleasure like rebounders do.

If I could get a rebound like that, just one, my whole life, I sure would smile. Paul didn't want it. He had the tools that made him a basketball player. I guess he wanted a different set of tools. Funny, funny—I sat there wanting his.

Why couldn't there be a way to trade? And why

couldn't I have something to trade him?

The only real intensity he showed was on defense. On offense, he just took up space and moved listlessly. On defense, whenever anyone tried to drive through the lane, he got there first, went up, and swatted the ball with a fury. He didn't just block it, he mashed it, as if he could one time hit it so hard that it wouldn't come back.

I found him so riveting to watch, I didn't notice right off who the point guard was, feeding Paul the ball time after time. It was Mikie. I'd never seen him like this. He ran the floor, he barked out plays, he called defensive assignments. And everyone listened to him. I watched the coach watching Mike. *My* Mike. He kept writing on his pad, whispering to his assistant, nodding, stroking his chin, clapping. Mikie penetrated and scooped in a layup. Mikie made a steal, Mikie stuck a jumper. Mikie threaded a pass through traffic to Paul. Paul passed it back out. Mikie passed it back in, harder. Paul threw it back out again. Mikie threw a bullet right into Paul's hands that must have stung. Paul's chest expanded double as he jumped straight up and *jammed* the ball in through two defenders.

Mikie was a monster. I had never seen this. But somehow I knew it. Shooting twenty-one in his driveway, Mikie always managed to beat me by just a few points. One on one with Frankie, who was a lot taller and pretty good, Mike'd still win by a few. In gym class at school, when Mike was playing against a so-so player, Mike was a little better than so-so. Then, when mighty David Myers came into the game, Mikie became *great*. The level of

42

competition. Mike had a gift for always playing above it. He never seemed to want to play way above it.

And there it was. He was doing it to the whole of our new school. I always figured we would get to a level Mikie would not be able to exceed. Half figured this would be it. It wasn't. It wasn't even in sight.

You'd think I'd be loving it. Shouldn't his best friend have been loving it?

I couldn't watch anymore, so I left.

It was a few hundred yards downhill to the pool. The sun beat on my face all the way, and I thought about how nice it might be to take a swim. There was a bubble dome over the pool building, and glass walls at either end, making it kind of like swimming outdoors. I peered in through the glass blocks, my mouth watering at the thought of all that cool water. Even the chlorine smell, so strong it seeped outside the building, had a kind of refreshing something attached to it.

Until, pressing hard into the glass, I saw how much fun this wasn't. I forgot, floating in my temporary freedom, that everything here has a purpose, and that fun is *not* that purpose. The swimmers locked in the cauldron of the Swimming Sector were working harder than anyone I'd seen in camp up to that point. The coach's whistle screeched like a cat under a car wheel every twenty seconds as he beat on them, pushing the boys through the water. He knew he had one of the prize Sectors, and let them all know it.

"You wanna swim? Or you wanna go out there and

run cross-country in the hot sun?" he yelled into the ear of a skinny blond boy bobbing lifelessly in the water. " 'Cause with your body, those are your choices. There's already a long waiting list for this Sector, and with all the football and baseball washouts pounding on the door tomorrow . . . you just better give me a stronger butterfly than the one you're givin' me."

My mouth hung open. I was at a summer camp in the middle of July where you could not swim. And staring in there, even with the sun crisping my neck, I didn't want to. Everyone in the pool, splashing madly away, looked to be sweating.

There was one place I felt confident of getting comfort. The dining hall. I found a new well of strength as I sweated my way up the long hill to that big chalet in the sky, with its American, Vatican, Massachusetts, and Knights flags huffing away against the clouds. The Knight was silver on a field of red, with a monstrous lance. Made the Native American on the Massachusetts flag look even more naked and in jeopardy than usual.

When I got to the dining hall, I found it taken up with a gaggle of wrestlers. All over, guys were just flinging one another to the floor, crashing and grunting so hard and in such numbers that the building vibrated like a Jell-O house. I took one look and turned right around.

I didn't even stop at the Track-and-Field Sector because the smell of sweat was so strong even from a hundred yards away.

I'd seen enough. The camp was everything I'd imagined it would be. I was heading back to my Cluster to have a well-earned lie-down when I found the Sector I wasn't even looking for. The Sector I never even suspected. The Secret Sector. There, isolated at the far end of the compound, past the administration building and the library, and the four seminarians' dormitory building that could house eighty, I heard the strangest noise.

Laughter.

This, I had to see.

When I turned the corner of the last building and passed through the small woods on the other side, I came to a clearing that was like changing countries. Two squads, a total of twelve students, combined with almost that many counsellors and coaches, strolled around in what could best be described as the Country Club Sector. Officially, the Golf and Tennis Sector, or GolTenSec.

Golf and tennis! They had a manicured nine-hole course hard by two clay courts. Everybody smiled and joked. Nobody hit anybody else. Not on the head, not in the gut. There was no leg whipping. There were no takedowns of any kind. These guys on the right would hit, but only fuzzy little yellow balls. Those off to the left would hit a little harder, but only dimpled little white balls. They were all tanned already.

How the hell did a guy rate GolTenSec? That's what I wanted to know.

I was going to find out, because right there in the

middle of it all, telling the jokes, getting the laughs, running the whole party as he bopped between both groups, was my old buddy Frankie.

I crept away before they could see me, all those long-legged, pearly-toothed, white-shoed, eerily happy little ball smackers. Like a daylight coven.

"What do you mean, how do I rate? Elvin, I'm a great tennis player, and an even better golfer." Frankie was lying on his bed after dinner, stretched out with his hands cupped behind his head. Looking kingly. I stood at the foot of his bed, dripping. I'd just come out of the shower—the *community* shower, gasp—and hadn't bothered to comb my hair or completely dry off. I stood with my towel tied around me like a skirt.

"Come on, Frank. You're not that good. You're okay, but you're better at other stuff, like baseball for one, and hockey for another."

He smiled. "You're right, Elvin. I'm not that good."

"So?"

He sat up, all earnest all of a sudden—and earnest is not one of Frank's natural modes. "All right, Elvin, I've been trying to explain this to you already. It's just, like, I *fit* here, know what I mean? Like I said before, this new world, all the older stuff—it fits me better than kid stuff ever did. I don't know why, but I just knew that I could do what I wanted to here, that I could get my way. And I do. But it's no mystery, man. I get what I want because I act like I expect it. Confidence. Act like you don't give a shit about anything, and they give you everything."

The things Frank said, the things he knew, were so far away from me that I couldn't even start to try to follow him. I knew that they just didn't, and never would, apply to me.

"Forget I asked," I said, and turned away. "Enjoy the country club."

"Wait a minute," he said.

I stopped, and as soon as I turned, somebody snuck up from my blind side. Whoever it was took a mighty two-handed yank on my towel, trying to rip it off.

I've spent my life expecting that—at YMCA camp, at school, at my cousins' summer cottage—so I was not unprepared. My knees buckled with the force of the pull, but my iron-rolled towel held. A second guy then came up, and the two of them pulled in opposite directions. It peeled open like stage curtains.

It sounded like a girlie show. High-pitched whistles, screams.

"Holy . . ."

"Get a *look* at that sucker."

"Jesus, save me, it's hideous. What'd you get, your thing tattooed?"

I didn't look around to see one single laughing face. I didn't try to retrieve my towel. I stared straight ahead, over Frankie, into a knot on the pine-paneled wall. Waiting for it all to go away.

Frankie jumped up on his bed. First he threw me his towel from the top of his locker. Then he stood there, staring wickedly down on the people closest to me, while he unbuckled his own pants. Then he yanked them down in front.

"How 'bout this one?" he yelled, walking forward to be right in front of one of them. He started wiggling his hips and pelvic thrusting. Right at the guy's face level. "Whatsa matter, guys, you don't get outta the house enough? Is this what you came here for?" Frankie pressed on, coming an inch from touching the kid's face with it, until they all backed away without saying anything. The one with Frank in his face took longest to leave, and was purple when he did.

I wrapped Frank's towel around me. It was smaller than mine, so I had to hold it in place, and my belly lopped over.

Frankie tried to be calm as he took his spot reclining again, but he wasn't really. Those kinds of guys don't bother him—in fact he sort of is one of those kinds of guys—but he looked worried. Worried for me.

"I don't think I could be a fitter, Frankie," I said. "Not like you."

"Maybe you could," he said, but he said it very weakly.

"No, I can't."

"Well," he said, almost like an apology, but then definitely not one. "Well I *can*, Elvin. I will, you know."

"I know," I said into the floor as I walked toward my bunk. "I went by the Hoop Sector today. Mikie will fit too. Thanks for the towel, Frank." I saw my own towel on the floor a few beds away from mine. I didn't bend down to pick it up, just kicked it along and under my bed.

Mom,

Well, you're in luck. The football coach and I had a bit of a falling out. So if you ever do come back to claim me, there is a good chance I will go home with you. It was no big thing, just a little strategic difference about how exactly the squad should be run. Great minds will differ, now won't they?

On the other hand, I have become most popular with my shipmates. It's something to do with my MOLE. You remember my MOLE, don't you Mom? I guess I haven't had a chance to show you my MOLE lately, but picture it just like when I was a baby, only five *hundred* times larger and bluer. Well, due to my MOLE, all my disrobings—for showers, for bed, or just to escape the sweat crust I've built up before noon every day—have become popular activities. They are by far the most unifying community events here, much bigger than movie night or campfire time, although they are similar in that the guys do all link arms and sing *songs* at my MOLE, Mom. It's just a shame that it's only gargantuan and blue and fuzzy and not hot as well, or I'm sure there'd be marshmallows involved.

Wear sunblock 45 down on the Vineyard, Mom. We wouldn't want you getting too exposed too. Say hi to Chelsea Clinton for me.

Love,
Elvin Bigtop

Chapter 4

Take me out to the ball game, and pummel me.

I could only imagine.

"Morning, Thor, how's tricks?" I inquired brightly, though I felt something short of hopeful about the prospects. I was to be resentenced this morning to a new sports gulag.

Thor was authentically bright and chipper this morning as he sat on his bunk, reading a rather stunning magazine called *Great Big Ones*. But I don't think it was any great big ones that had him so up. It was me. He knew I was coming for reassignment this morning, and frankly Thor was beginning to really warm up to me. Every time we had a conversation, he looked ready to explode with laughter. He tossed *Great Big Ones* aside.

"Bish," he greeted me. "How the hell are ya?"

"Oh god, this is going to hurt real bad, isn't it?"

"Jeez, would you stop already? You're so gloomy all the time. Fact is, I worked my butt off and pulled you one plum assignment. You're gonna want to kiss me. But you can't."

I would not bite. I just stood, waiting, my hands folded in front of me.

"Baseball Sector," he said, beaming.

"Baseball Sector?"

He nodded. If he wasn't just toying with me because I was vulnerable, then he was right, this was a coup for him and a reprieve for me.

"I heard Baseball Sector was standing room only."

"I got seniority, so I got clout." He kicked back on his bed looking satisfied.

He had clout—even his bunk said that. He had an actual bed, with springs. He had the same kind of skinny locker we all had, but he had four of them pressed together. One of the seminarians actually came by every few days and picked up Thor's toxic laundry bag. That was power.

"You did that for me?" I said through a very twisted, skeptical expression.

"I did it for you."

Baseball. I never even dared dream it. Not that I had any knack for it, any skill at it, not that I had any affection for the game or the slightest contribution to make to it. I had nothing. In fact I had more nothing for baseball than all the nothings I had for other sports combined. A herculean nothing. But neither was I likely to get mauled during my stint in the Baseball Sector. Every kid knew this. That was why on day three, Baseball Sector was the hottest ticket in town. The waiting list was overflowing with soft kids seeking asylum after two days of full-contact war games.

There are so many bodies in baseball camp, nobody's got time to harass you much if you stink. You just take your three cuts, *whiff*, and get out of the way, because *everybody* is waiting to hit. You sit around in right field for a while, let one go through your legs, let a couple more go over your head, and you're out of there. Third base? Just show them your famous "hands of stone," catch the ball with your stomach, or—my favorite, guaranteed to get you the hook—duck when a line drive comes your way. On the off chance you actually get to and corral a grounder, throw it ten feet wide and into the brook. All of this, to me, was natural, and I never had to work at it.

It wasn't pretty, and it wasn't much fun, but it kept a guy off the line, out of harm's way, and reasonably comfortable. The equivalent of a minimum-security prison.

Unless.

"There is one, ah . . . well it's not a *catch*, exactly . . ."

Unless.

"Don't look that way, Bish. You can't expect such a great deal for nothing."

Unless.

Thor pulled it slowly from behind his pillow. The Mitt.

"No, Thor, no. You can't do this. I don't want to

catch. I can't catch. Why do I have to be catcher? I can't even get into that position—look." I went into a half squat, then abandoned it as I struggled back up with a mighty groan. "See? Won't work."

"I had to tell them you would. Nobody else'll do it. They had three catchers, and one of them broke his finger yesterday."

"First base. I can play first base. There is no law that says the fat kid has to play catcher. Look at that guy in Detroit. Cecil Somebody. Size of a house. I saw him on a Pizza Hut commercial or something. Isn't he a first baseman? And that guy on the Red Sox, very large, very large."

Thor just closed his eyes and shook his head. "Bish. It was the only way I could get you the slot. You gotta go."

He handed me the mitt solemnly, like an eviction notice or a last smoke. I took it. It was as big as a meat-serving platter, and very heavy.

The first half of the day was drills. First the pitcher drilled me in the kidney while I was batting. Then he drilled me in the face mask when I was behind the plate.

One of the impressive things about a baseball program is that there are so many micro coaches for all the fine skills. Basketball just has the basketball coach, and maybe a couple of assistant coaches. Baseball has a manager, a batting coach, a pitching coach, a third-base coach, a first-base coach, an infield coach, and a bullpen coach. And on *this* team, for today at least, they had a catcher's coach.

"Do something with him, will ya, Vinnie?" the coach yelled to one of the counsellors. "We got to scrimmage this afternoon, and he's gonna wreck the whole thing."

"First," Vinnie said, talking loudly, as if I were a moron rather than just out of shape, "you cannot *sit* on the ground behind the plate. Get up." I got up and followed Vinnie to what they called the "lower field," the raggedy, unkept practice diamond where players who needed remedial work were isolated so they wouldn't infect the healthy athletes.

When we were behind the stone home plate set into the ground of the old field, Vinnie painstakingly bent and forced my body down into the classic catcher pose. I held it, frozen like a baseball-card photo, while Vinnie went to the mound to pitch to me. Problem was, I had to hold my breath. Because if I let it out, my balance was so touch-and-go I knew I was going to roll backward.

I had to do it. I exhaled. I fell backward.

Vinnie didn't see it. He got to the mound and picked up the ball. When he spun toward me to start pitching, I was already laid out looking for the high fly ball in the sun.

"What are you doing?" he asked with what was quickly blossoming into full-flowered hatred.

"I'm stretching," I said. Fighting my chest protector, shin pads, and loose mask, I managed to roll onto my side, stand, and squat again.

He went into his windup. In the middle of it, at the top of his motion, I stood up.

"Time out," I called, my hand and mitt out in front of me.

"Jesus," he yelled, cutting his delivery in half. "What is your problem?"

"I'm sorry, I cannot manage that position. I'll just keep bowling over."

Vinnie slammed the ball into his mitt, then slammed the mitt down on the mound. He marched toward me like a batter charging the mound, only in reverse.

"Then try *this*," he barked, putting his hand on top of my head and pushing me down. He folded me again into a respectable catcher pose, then just before time ran out on my balance, he grabbed my right leg and yanked it straight out to the side. I was still crouched, but the extended leg stood out there like a brace. I tried leaning on it. It held, despite a creeping pain coming on in the hip socket. I didn't feel like I was going to tip over anymore. I had never had my leg out in that direction before, didn't even know it could be done. Except with a Barbie doll.

"You look good," Vinnie screamed from the mound. "You ready?"

I nodded, lying without even speaking. Vinnie reared back; his foot went way up in the air, above his head. His face disappeared behind his shoulder. He coiled, spun, unfolded toward the plate, slung the ball with a wicked snap of the wrist.

It was, judging from its behavior, a curveball. I watched it come toward me, spinning, humming. It started out way over there, came over here, went right on past over to there. The ball and I never met. It didn't get in my way, and I didn't get in its. I remained frozen in my perfect catcher's pose as the ball hit the backstop.

Vinnie glared toward me. Words failed him. Then he stormed off the mound, spitting, muttering, ". . . not putting up with this crap . . . not chasing balls all over the damn place all morning . . ."

He returned with a tin bucket filled with baseballs. "Crash course," he said, and went to work like an automatic pitching machine.

Vinnie was a guy who did not waste his few words. When he said, "Crash course," it was a gesture of sincerity. After an hour, I was no more prepared to catch a game of baseball than I had been when I first woke up that morning. But I was well prepared to get pelted by baseballs.

"Block the plate, kid. If nothing else, remember that blocking the plate is the bottom line of your job. You don't let the ball get by you, and you don't let a runner cross the plate without a rumble. Whoever or whatever tries to get across, you use . . . that body of yours to make sure it doesn't happen."

By now Vinnie and I had established a relationship where we could be frank with each other without jeopardizing our friendship.

"Now see, that doesn't make any sense to me at all. All my life I've been taught to get out of the way of speeding hard things that might kill me, and you think

57

I'm going to start doing the whole opposite thing now?"

He whistled the ball off my chest protector. "Yes I do," he said.

The balls bounced off my shin pads—god, I learned to love those shin pads—off my mask, off my unprotected shoulders, and occasionally off my glove. Against my better judgment I learned to aim my body at the ball when I saw it coming, to the point where better than fifty percent of the balls didn't get by. I got a lot better at it when I realized it was much more exhausting to chase the ball to the backstop every time than to just let it thunk into me.

"Fine, you're ready," Vinnie said when his arm started to tire and yet another of my throws landed softly in the turf six feet short of the mound.

"That's it?" I asked, gratefully stripping the mask from my baking face. "You going to throw me batting practice now? I can't hit, either, you know."

"Did you bat earlier?"

"Three pitches. Five counting the two that hit me. I thought maybe you'd show me more."

He looked at me as if I'd just asked him to cook me dinner. "What are you, *joking*? You had to learn to catch so you didn't hold up the game. Hitting? Just take your cuts and get the hell outta the way."

"Sounds good to me, Coach," I said as I settled my face in under the Gatorade cooler that sat on the bench. I opened my mouth and the spigot and let it pour in. Vinnie started walking back to the big field to carry forth the lie that I was ready to play ball.

The real pitcher, even though he was just a kid, threw a lot harder than Vinnie did. His name was Smoke. I don't imagine that was his real name, but we never got deep enough into conversation to talk about it. Mostly we talked in signs.

I wiggled my fingers between my legs. One down for fastball, two for curve. First pitch I signaled number two. He threw a fastball so hard it took my glove off and carried it back to the umpire.

I signaled two again. Fastball. I couldn't even catch up with it. Bounced off my shin pads.

I signaled two again.

"Time out," Smoke called. Play was halted, and he waved me to the mound for a conference. "What the hell are you doing with your fingers down there?"

"I'm calling the game. Those are the signs, one finger for fastball, two for curve."

"I got a sign for you," he said, and gave me one. One finger, up. Rotating. "You're a friggin' backstop, kid. Don't tell me what to throw."

I slunk back to my station, the one cool thing about catching ripped away from me. There was nothing left but the sweat and facelessness the padding gave me, and all that work. Next to pitcher, catcher is the only one who works all the time. Catch the ball, throw the ball, block the ball, throw the ball. Even on foul balls I had to jump up, throw the mask, search the sky for the ball. Invariably, I was the last one to pick up on it, and everyone would be back in position waiting for me while I wandered around clueless like Robert De Niro near the end of *Bang the Drum Slowly.*

I was exhausted by the second inning. Fortunately, nobody could hit Smoke, so there weren't many base runners to worry about. Just a couple of guys he hit on purpose. Both of them stole second, then third, one of my throws to second being so lame that Smoke caught it.

My glove hand was so pink and raw and swollen from Smoke's perfectly placed fastballs that I couldn't have missed if I wanted to.

In the third inning I got to hit. No, that's a lie. In the third inning, I got to stand in the box with a bat on my shoulder. Fastball. *Pop!* in the glove. Steee-rike one. Fastball. Steee-rike two. I dug in. I was going to swing at this thing at least once. I couldn't react quickly enough, so I had to anticipate, not wait for the ball. He wound up, came over the top, and as soon as he let go of the ball, I started my swing.

I swung as ferociously as I could, throwing myself so wildly off balance and ahead of the ball that I watched from the ground as the pitch floated about a foot outside. "Well, what do you know?" I thought, suspended in another one of life's fabulous, cruel slo-mo moments. "A curve ball. Imagine that."

The opposing team hooted me. I looked to my own side of the field to see my team with all their heads down as they took the field, trying not to laugh or get angry. That was embarrassing.

The thing I couldn't seem to remember was that, with

all the equipment on, I was fairly protected from a pitch bouncing up out of the dirt. Out of reflex, I kept turning my face away as I stabbed at it with the glove.

"Cut that out," I kept hearing Vinnie scream. "Keep your eye on the ball."

I heard him and I heard him and I heard him, but I just could not get my body to obey. In the fourth inning I paid. Smoke put a real hard one in the dirt, bouncing it right on the plate so that it ricocheted up like a super ball. I closed my eyes and turned my face halfway away as I tried to spear it, but it came up and blasted me.

I don't know what it sounded like outside my own head, but inside, when the hardball hit my jaw, it didn't sound any different from when the bat hits the ball. It blew me over backward, and I flopped around, mask and glove flying off in opposite directions.

I heard laughs. Not everyone, but quite a few. Problem was, I got right up. I was rubbing and rubbing at the spot, moving my jaw all around to test it. So since I wasn't dead, it was funny.

Coach called from the sidelines, "You all right, kid?"

I nodded. He didn't care. I didn't care.

But the batter and the umpire came up to me, looked closely at my jaw. Their eyes were big and deep, like real human eyes. They both asked if I was all right, and they meant it. Because they had been close, and they had heard it.

Why do people have to hear the bone smash before they can care?

I went back to work and did all right. I only had a headache. The heat and the squatting and the catching and catching and catching every pitch was beating me down. I drank all the Gatorade they'd allow me between innings. There was always a line at the cooler. When it was my turn, I took my cup to the back of the line and drank while I waited for more. I heard guys around me talking baseball, but I couldn't. I couldn't because I didn't know baseball. And I couldn't because I couldn't talk.

There was, unfortunately, a rally. Just as I had gotten all my gear back on, I had to strip it off again. I put on my helmet and went to the plate.

The first pitch was coming right at me. I bailed out of the batter's box. The ball bailed the other way. Steee-rike.

The second pitch was coming right at me. I waited a bit longer this time, then fell backward. Like a bowling ball spinning across the lane, the ball went the other way again. Steee-rike two.

I could not, and never would, not if I faced ten thousand of them a day, fathom the curve ball. All I could hope was to outguess it.

The next pitch came my way, but I wasn't going anywhere. Even when I realized it had a lot more on it than the previous two. It was going to break, it was going to break. I was not going to look foolish again, dammit. Break, ball.

Of course, it never broke. That's what setting up the batter is all about. As a catcher I was supposed to understand that.

They say that the hardest thing to do in all of sports is to hit a baseball. I say the hardest thing to do is to get out of the way of one after guessing wrong.

The ball caromed off my helmet, back out all the way to the shortstop. Better than if I'd hit it with the bat.

Mostly I was stunned, not hurt. I trotted to first, and was pretty pleased to be there. The first baseman slapped my butt, and I felt a little bit a part of it all.

The next batter hit a rocket into the left centerfield gap. The runner scored from third. The man on second motored all the way around and scored easily.

For twenty seconds or whatever it took, I put more effort into running than I'd ever put into something physical before. The other runners were in, and there was me. I desperately wanted not to kill the rally, but I kept running and running and second base just wouldn't come any closer. I saw the left fielder wheel and throw toward second. I chugged, feeling all the parts of my body shaking, my hat blowing off. I felt something behind me, the hitter, who was about to run up my back until he realized he had to go back.

I flopped, threw myself at the bag, kicked up a mushroom cloud of dirt as I slid facefirst. It was a mess, but I was there.

"You're out," the umpire said matter-of-factly. I was shocked, but apparently I was out by enough distance that the fielders were already trotting off the field when the ump raised his thumb.

It took a long time to get myself out of the dirt. It

turned instantly to mud on my face, neck and arms, mixed with the sweat. Guys ran off the field, guys walked or ran on. I trudged slowly, trying to tuck in my shirt as I went, trying to find my hat. When I eventually reached the bench, the coach was strapping on the catcher's gear.

"You want to call it a day, son?" It was not unkind, the way he said it. But it didn't seem to come easy either.

"I guess so," I said.

So I got my wish. The vision of sitting on the bench, kicked back, scratching, spitting, yelling "Hummm baby," and "No batter up there," and sipping Gatorade without waiting in line and chewing on sunflower seeds—it was mine now.

It wasn't ten tons of fun, but it was peaceful and relaxing. I watched the final few innings, but I could not say what went on, who won, if Smoke got his no-hitter. What I could say is that the field had a strong smell of chamomile, coming from a big patch in right field, and that a total of twelve puffy clouds lazed across the front of the sun, and that two of them looked like my old fat dog Sheba, and one looked like a convertible Mustang with an infant at the wheel.

As I filed off the field, thinking this was not the worst thing that could happen to a guy, the coach—now he was the one looking wiped out from catching—called in my direction. But he was talking to Vinnie.

"Vin, put a splint on that kid with the finger. I want him back here tomorrow."

Mom,

Got transferred to a more gentlemanly sport today, baseball. No contact. Good, right? Couple of bruises anyway, because, well, I'm gifted at that. Some regular hit-in-the-coconut injuries, and some others that I can't talk about in mixed company. You'd have to be a catcher to understand.

The bonk on the head didn't hurt much, so don't worry. You weren't, were you? Worrying? Oh, good.

Did I mention that I played baseball today? A more gentlemanly sport than football, I think.

My head doesn't hurt at all. I did get bonked, though.

How's the wife and kids?

So I hope I can count on your support in November.

I played soccer all day today. I scored many goals. Sheba was there too.

Sincerely,
um,
ah,
hnn,

Chapter 5

Grappling Knight

The baseball door closed as abruptly as it had opened. New day, new slot, new Elvin. By decree. "Wrestling, Thor? How do you come up with that?"

"There were a lot of casualties the last two days out of wrestling. Slots are open. Besides, it's the only program that actually has a category with your name on it: Junior Heavyweight."

"Come on, don't you have anything else?"

"Sure," he said, smiling. "I could squeeze you into Swimming Sector, but you gotta wear this." Out of his breast pocket Thor produced a Lycra Speedo bathing suit, grape with diagonal lime-green lightning bolts. He pulled it down over his fist, and it fit snugly.

"One size fits all," he said, smirking.

"I should," I said, sounding almost like I meant it. "It'd serve you all right, to look at me in that thing. I'd wear it to all the meals."

He continued to hold it out to me.

"Where do I get my wrestling gear?" I moaned.

"At the venue." He pointed up the hill to the hall.

When I turned to go, I was surprised to feel Thor's arm on me. He gripped my forearm hard and pulled me back.

"Elvin, I want to give you some advice. You're a funny kid, and I like you. You don't take the whole slotting thing seriously, and that's cool, but for your own sake just try to take it a little *more* seriously. Try to find a place. I don't want to say nothing bad about the school now, but it could be a long four years for a guy if he doesn't have a place. Know?"

He looked so serious, as if he was telling me of a death in the family, that he gave me a chill. I couldn't answer him, couldn't really tell if he'd even asked me anything.

"Just a *little* more seriously, that's all. It's better for a guy like you, in a big school. You want to have a place. You *don't* want to not have a place. Just advice. Okay, Elvin?"

That time, it sounded like a question. "Okay," I said, because Thor seemed to want to help me. But I didn't know what I could do with that advice.

When I walked up the steps of the dining hall, under the poor semi-naked Massachusetts Indian that I was staring at more and more, I felt my stomach knot.

"Ah, and in they continue to roll," the perfect coach announced. In a crowd of a thousand people you would point to this man—hard and energetic and crew cut—and say this guy is a wrestling coach. "The traditional day-three football washouts," he said, up on his toes and gesturing as he spoke. "Am I right?"

"You are right," I said. "Except I'm a two-day football washout via a one-day layover in baseball."

"Catcher!" Coach said, excited by his own savvy.

"Catcher it was," I said.

"Well, son, I do hope you find a home here with the Grappling Knights. We'd love to have you."

He was a little corny, but he sounded all right. My stomach briefly unballed. Then I got a load of the grunting, grappling Knights.

In a weird way it was as if I had made a wish and found it had been granted. When Thor held up that Speedo, one size fits all, I shrank inside, feeling like that was the farthest thing from what I needed now. So instead I wound up with the wrestling squad, whose motto should have been all sizes fit one sport.

It made sense when I saw them. Unlike other sports, I was assigned this one because I *fit*. The wrestling team had a built-in slot for me—junior heavyweight—just like Thor said. And they have slots for a lot of other freaks too. It was a world defined purely by weight, the first thing that was clearly laid out since I got here.

It was probably rude, the way I stood in the middle of the floor and stared at them before getting too close. But the way they were so relaxed about it, I figured I wasn't the first. Some of them just flopped, several stretched out their legs and arms, bending and kicking and wind-milling as if they were already at work, battling some invisible opponents. A couple of tight, compact, round-muscled guys did this thing where they locked arms back to back and took turns lifting each other off the floor. They enjoyed it so much, they took the show on the road, lifting, walking, dropping the other guy, then being lifted, walked, dropped, until they made a circuit of the whole hall.

The world of weight. *I* was merely a junior heavy-weight. Which meant that above me were two more weight classes: heavyweight and super heavyweight. And for practice purposes they tried to have two of each on hand, which meant this group had several people even *bigger* than my last club.

Below the heaviest weights were the real athletes: middleweights, junior middleweights, welterweights. These guys were the cat family, coiled, edgy, muscled, with a thin layer of flesh strapped tight over the sinew. They were mean, and could have played with the football or hockey teams if they had wanted to, except those sports didn't allow the close personal head twisting and leg bending so popular in wrestling. Not to mention, of course, the pinning of another guy by forcing his legs up over his head.

The bottom tier of grappling Knights was more mot-ley than all the others. Featherweights, bantamweights, flyweights. The titles pretty much say it all. At the Olympic level you might see a tiny guy who is scary and intense and strong, who just happens to be small boned. But in the general population, when they're just trying to fill the slot of "peanuttiest little guys," the result is a collection of skeletons, anemics, and leprechauns who might possibly be able to scare the chess team, but also might not.

At the top of the ladder we had an honest-to-god giant. Not a great big guy, but a guy with some kind of gland thing that made his head the same width as his hips and his hands the size of stop signs.

At the bottom we had a dwarf. A very mean, stocky three-foot-nine bantam.

"Here ya go, man," the coach said brightly, tossing me my one-piece outfit. His name, written in marker across the front of his tight T-shirt, was Coach Wolfe.

I took the outfit into the dressing room/equipment room/kitchen and strapped it on. It was like one of those old-timey bathing suits guys like Charlie Chaplin and The Great Gatsby used to wear, with the squared-off legs and the thin shoulder straps. It was red, of course. I felt naked, shuffling back into the main dining hall, the way the stretchy material clung to the rolling terrain of me and blended with the rosy pinkness of my embarrassed skin tone.

And it crawled. I pulled it out. It crawled back up. I stretched the straps as far as possible to relieve some of the tension. They snapped back up. By the time I'd crossed the whole floor to where the team was assembled, they were all watching my crab-walking–cheek-squeezing–pick-the-thong-out-of-my-butt dance.

"Hey, man, synchronized swimming is down at the pool," one guy called, bringing hoots of laughter. I sized him up as he smirked at me. He was a junior heavyweight, of course. Only *his* fat seemed to come with some muscles.

It was about evenly divided between guys who were there because they were real wrestlers and wanted to be on the school team and guys who were there just because, well, everybody's got to be somewhere. My partner, the smart-mouth guy, was a wrestler wrestler.

"Okay, Bishop, Metzger, square off. Let's see what we got now in junior heavy. It's been pretty boring for poor ol' Metz up till now."

"How unfortunate," I thought as I reluctantly approached the center of the mat. "My opponent has been bored, waiting for me. He's had nobody his own size to pick on for three whole days."

The other wrestlers gathered around the edges of the mat. Metzger stood across from me, two feet of very thin air separating us. He crouched, staring right into my eyes. I wished I was back in football. I crouched and could see my hands trembling on my knees. I thought about Frankie, for some reason. Wished he was here. Mikie too. I felt like I wanted to run. A feeling that came over me *very* infrequently. I couldn't do that, I knew. So when Wolfe screeched the whistle, I blasted straight ahead.

I had no idea. All this time, and I never even knew.

But now, pushed to the wall, I found out about myself, as many others in history have found their own hidden greatness, through adversity. I found my niche: I was a *great* wrestler.

With my initial burst, I drove Metzger backward. He was stunned by my aggressiveness. I pressed the attack, taking advantage of the situation the way all great strategists must. I blasted him again. He looked to the sidelines, stunned, for help. Too bad, Metz. I grabbed him. I twisted him. I bent him to my will.

"What the f—" he yelped.

Power like nothing else I'd ever known surged through my body. I wanted to wrestle, and I never wanted to stop wrestling.

So I didn't. Metzger, beaten into cowardice, had his back to me by the time I caught him for the final destruction. I laughed out loud. Metzger gurgled in my grip.

I felt the footsteps pounding toward me from three sides. They'd be hoisting me to their shoulders any second. The messiah of the wrestling program.

There was a scream. "You can't do that!"

I continued to squeeze Metzger's windpipe.

Hands were all over me then. "You can't do that!" There was that scream again.

I gouged the eye. I bit the top of his head.

"Cut that out. Stop it. Stop right now." That was the coach. He joined three others in dragging me off, all pinning me down at once. Only then, looking into the coach's soft black eyes, did I get it.

Apparently, I had the wrong kind of wrestling.

"I *can't*?" I asked, when things had quieted down. I was back in the dressing kitchen, where Coach Wolfe was just now giving me the orientation he *should* have given me before.

"I can't punch?"

He shook his head in disbelief. I was starting to get very familiar with this reaction around camp.

"I can't kick? I can't do the scissors, or the iron claw?"

He laughed. "I almost wish you could, Bishop. You're bringing back some memories for me. But unfortunately no, this is a different kind of wrestling."

"Well jeez, somebody could have *told* me," I said, a little perturbed. Then I sank into a confidential whisper, as if what I told him next was a big secret. "Frankly, Coach, I'm not really a sports guy. I'm a TV guy. As far as I'm concerned, what I was doing was wrestling. I don't know what the hell you people are doing." I stared through a kitchen window, out to where the rest of the guys were practicing. "Look at that. One guy starts out on his hands and knees, and the other guy gets to jump on him. Does that seem fair to you?"

Coach walked up and slapped me on the back of the neck. It hurt like hell, but the look on his face indicated it was a friendly, sports-guys gesture, so I didn't mind too much. With that kindly grip on my brain stem, he guided me back out to the floor. "Yes, actually it does, but you have to understand the game first. The real game. We'll get you some coaching," he said. "You'll be all right."

First order of business in my rehabilitation was apologizing to Metzger.

"Sorry, Metzger," I mumbled, although the sight of him still sitting slumped, rubbing his chafed throat, gave me a little rush all over again.

"Ya," he grunted. "Well, it didn't hurt anyway, except when you were scratching."

"I never scratched you."

"Yes you did, blob."

"Oh ya, I'll do it again if you don't watch—" I pulled to get out of Coach's grip, but he held me with three fingers without even trying too hard.

"We'll pair you up with somebody else for a while," Coach Wolfe said.

The somebody else turned out to be Eugene the Giant. In the all-important nickname industry within juvenile athletics, Eugene was known as "Eugene No-Hygiene." At first I thought, "How cruel." Until I worked, closely, with the guy for a day. He'd earned that nickname. By the second day I was a better wrestler simply because Eugene offended me so much. Did he change that underwear between days one and two? Legitimate question. Did he use deodorant? Not even a question. He was tough to get a hold on because of the thick layer of oil that laminated his entire person, from the top of his gargantuan, matted head along the whitehead-peaked range of his face to his long reptilian arms and legs. His coating was thick and unbreakable, like the Skin-So-Soft my mother used to slather all over me to keep the mosquitoes away. But it didn't smell like Skin-So-Soft. No, no it did not smell like Skin-So-Soft.

The very worst of it was I liked Eugene. He was a big, powerful, gentle mutant bear, and he went out of his way to try and teach me some of what he knew about the sport. Which was considerable.

He kept setting me up in all the positions, teaching me how to break the hold or to press the attack.

"Here, put your hand here, on my wrist," he said as he planted himself four on the floor. "The other arm around my waist. This knee up, the other one down." He spoke slowly, the same way he walked, his legs and his words both unfolding gradually but determinedly. I put the hold on him.

"Spread your legs wider," he said.

"I am."

"No, wider, your balance is no good."

"I can't. That's it."

"You have to. Stretch."

"Eugene, my legs are already further apart than they've ever been before. I'm afraid they're traumatized with the whole separation thing."

Eugene's hands were a lot quicker than his feet or his speech. When it was clear I would not improve my balance, his left hand stabbed out behind him, seized my lower leg, and pulled. The leg came out from under me, he pushed my upper body backward with his, and I found myself *thunk* on the floor. When I hit, Eugene hit with me, pinning me, his glistening broad back pressed hard against my chest. He still held the leg, and used it to lever me to the floor.

"Get your shoulders up," he grunted. "Don't let me pin your shoulders to the floor." It was almost comical, but that's just what he was like. Straining to do something to me, while at the same time trying to teach me to stop him from doing it.

I tried. I pushed with whatever strength I had, but Eugene had all the angle. He had spread his big frame out in all directions, getting both feet and one hand flat on the floor, so that in addition to his strength and weight, his balance made it like trying to lift a gigantic manhole cover off of me.

"I can't, Eugene."

"Then get one shoulder up. Come on, Elvin," he yelled. "Concentrate on nothing but the ball of that one shoulder, focus on it, that you will *not* let anybody get that shoulder down on the mat. You got one thing, one piece of ground to hold, and nobody's gonna take it from you."

He was so earnest, so intense, that I had to follow his directions. I heaved, filling my head with blood as I pushed. But I got it up there. A couple inches of space opened between the floor and my right shoulder.

"Good, Elvin, good. Excellent," Eugene said, sounding truly excited for me. I was actually making him work. Unfortunately I was making him sweat as well. Warmed, he smelled like boiling cabbage. He pushed back, slammed me back down.

I wriggled, got the other shoulder up now.

"Great move," he said. "You're still alive. Stay alive. That's the thing. As long as you get it up off the mat, you're alive. And as long as you're still alive . . . you never know. Anything can happen."

I fed on that. It wasn't winning, certainly, being ninety percent pinned, but there was a certain amount of victory in this, holding my ground, hanging in. I was determined that I would.

"Whew," Eugene said suddenly. "What a stench. Was that you, Elvin?"

"No," I squeezed through gritted teeth, trying to save my little remaining breath.

"Oh ya," he said. "I forgot. It was me."

I laughed first, and as soon as I did, all the strength ran out. I fell back and lay flattened, Eugene laughing and finishing off the pin with his shoulder blades.

"That wasn't bad," he said, standing over me. I still lay exhausted but satisfied and flat on my back. "I guess what we have to do with you is teach you in reverse. We start with you down for the count, try to get you un-pinned, then off the mat, then maybe competitive. . . ." He held his hand out to me.

"Let's not get too ambitious," I said.

He pulled me up off the floor, and just as I reached upright position, my shoulder popped out of its socket. I wailed. Eugene checked it out, squeezed my embarrass-ingly soft shoulder, worked his fingers in toward the joint as if he was kneading pizza dough.

"Ah, there," he said, gave it a little bang, and knocked it back into place.

"Thanks," I said. It was better, though it still hurt a lot.

"You better go let the nurse look at you," Eugene said.

"What's wrong?" Coach Wolfe asked, making his rounds.

"Elvin's got a—"

"Bruise," I said, elbowing him. "No big deal, Coach."

"Ah, you'll have plenty of those, Elvin," Coach said, punching the shoulder. He didn't notice the tears this brought to my eyes. Eugene did.

"You sure you don't want to go to sick bay?"

I was sure I did not want to go to sick bay. It was the fifth day of camp, and the first time I felt like I didn't want to sleep the whole thing off on the injured list. I hurt, and I was more than a little nervous about what else was in store for my unprepared body, but for a change I felt like I might actually be getting somewhere.

"I'm fine, Eugene," I said, windmilling my shoulder slowly.

"Okay, that's it, just don't let it stiffen up. You're doin' right, Elvin. When you're ready, we'll do some more. I'll show you about balance, about keeping your big butt off the floor. Just don't get stiff. That's it. Don't stiffen up now."

Ma,

I suppose this is what you wanted, so don't go bawling your eyes out. I just want you to know that

78

things are happening here. Changes by the hour, and you might not recognize your baby.

Remember you told me not to get in any fights? I fight every single day. So what do you think of that? Several *times* a day. And I'm enjoying it.

Hey, here's something I learned. Do you know what enuresis is? I do now, because the nurse explained it to me. It's something that happens to you when the coach announces that tomorrow you'll be fighting the guy with the axe scar across his whole cheek.

Do you know what an exercise mat tastes like? I do. But it depends who's been sliding around on it before your mouth gets pressed into it. It does not taste like chicken.

Remember those carnival people you pointed out never to associate with? What do you know, they've all turned up in my Sector. Every morning we meet, strip together, pull on tights, then spend the rest of the day rolling around on the floor together.

They have mass here two times a day, but they have no confession, so I'm afraid it may be too late by the time I get home.

Send postage, and I'll send you an 8 x 10.

Elvin "The Body" Bishop

PART 2
WEEK TWO

Chapter 6

Some pain, some gain.

"What's wrong with your arm?" Frankie asked at Nightmeal, his wide-open mouth full of watery mashed potatoes. The potatoes were so thin, you could see through them like lemon slush.

"Nothing," I said, picking my left arm off the table with my right hand and letting it fall to my side.

"Looks a little weak to me," Mikie said.

"Weaker than usual even," Frank said. He threw a fish puff in the air like a grape and swallowed it after chewing twice.

"Ya, well it's *stronger* than usual even, if you really want to know," I said, leaning over the table toward Frank.

"Whoa, I give up, I give up." Frank put his hands up in front of his face. "Mikie, do you believe what's happening to this guy? That wrestling thing's making a real menace out of him."

Mikie nodded while at the same time drinking milk out of the little carton. He finished and opened another one. "I know it. He's getting pretty fearsome"—he tipped a glance down at my lower regions—"and large."

"Dammit, Mike, would you please leave me alone." I looked away, at nothing in particular, but he was right. The first real physical activity of my life was actually making me *fatter*. I was famished all the time.

"You going to finish that?" I asked, pointing at Frank's briquette of corn bread. He rolled it off his tray toward mine. I scooped it up and bit it. It sounded like an apple.

"You lifting weights, El?" Mike asked.

"Some."

"You running?"

I got some corn bread granules stuck in my nose laughing at that one.

"Maybe you should run a little. Just for a balanced program."

"Listen, I appreciate your interest, Mike, but I have to remain strong. Look at this." I gave him the traditional Muscle Beach one-biceps flex.

"I don't see it, El," Frankie said, straining to get a look.

"I don't either," Mikie said.

I looked at it myself. I didn't see it either. I let it go slack, then tightened it again. There, there was a difference.

"Give it a squeeze," I said. They both did. Then they

nodded, but they had to sort of fish around in there to find it.

"Still," Mikie said, "it might be good to get some cardiovascular action, you know, just so . . ."

"So you don't have a heart attack," Frank finished.

"Don't worry about me—I'm fine. Anyway, I have to keep my weight up, or I won't be a junior heavyweight anymore."

"Gonna be a senior heavyweight pretty soon," Mike said.

"Yo, Franko," Obie, the senior football stud, said, putting both hands on Frankie's shoulders.

"Hey, Obie," Frank gushed. "What's happening?"

"You wanna come out tomorrow night? We're goin' out."

I looked at Mikie at the same time Mikie looked at me. Then we both turned and looked at Obie. Obie was one of the upperclassmen I had seen down in the clearing with Frank. A very big muck among mucks around here. He was a football star at the school but didn't bother much with the Football Sector here. He mostly marched around camp just being awesome and too cool. The way football stars do.

"Out?" Frank asked. "What kind of out? They don't let me out."

Obie laughed. "Just out. Me and some of the other counsellor boys just thought we'd get out for a while, stretch our legs. But don't worry. You're with us, then nobody's got a problem with it, I guarantee."

Frank turned back to us. We both shrugged.

"Sounds like fun," Frank said up over his shoulder. Obie loomed over him like a big square billboard for beef. "How 'bout them?" Frank asked, meaning us.

Obie looked our way, made a sour face. "No way," he said.

I was relieved, actually. Mike showed no feeling about it one way or the other.

"Ah, it's movie night tomorrow anyhow," Frank said, but he looked pained saying it. "Maybe I'll just hang out here."

Obie's lips tightened. I guessed Obie wasn't used to hearing no. "Y'know, if you *gotta* have your little friends with ya, I s'pose you can bring 'em," he said.

Frank's face brightened. "Okay, Obie, let me talk to them, and I'll catch you later."

"Okay, good. I'll be there at the movies, and when the lights go out we take off."

"Cool," Frankie said, offering up a flat palm above his head for Obie to slap.

"He's not there anymore," Mike said.

Frankie pulled the hand down. "Oh. Well anyway, he's great. Him, and his boys too. You guys are really lucky. This is a major social move here, to be hanging out with them."

"Ah . . . I don't know . . ." I started.

"You *can't* say no," Frank insisted.

"Well," Mikie said, "let's just give it a try. Ummmm . . . *No*. See, there, I can so say it."

Frank got desperate. "Hey, you guys. I worked hard. You saw. . . . How can you just turn it down? Don't embarrass me now."

Mike enjoyed this. "Hey, Franko, the movie might be great. Might be a *must see*. If it is, then I *must* see it. Elvin, you know what the movie is tomorrow night?"

"Ya, I think it's *Ernest Goes to Camp*."

"Oh, see that, Frankie, it's out of my hands now. *Ernest Goes to Camp*. Need I say more?"

"Stop it. You'll go, right?" Frank said hopefully. "I'm not joking now. I mean, I want to get in the right circle, that's key, but I always figured you guys were coming with me. You know, like we all jump together, and it'll be the best, right?"

Mikie picked up his tray and started toward the trash barrel. "Hmmm," he said, faking deep thought. I could tell he was jerking Frankie a little. Frankie could have seen too, if he was thinking okay.

"You didn't even touch the pound cake," I said, dashing, more or less, after Mikie. Frank followed right behind me.

"I'd like to all jump together," Mike said, "but I don't know if I want to jump where you want to jump, Frank. Let me think about it." That seemed to be good enough for Frank for now. It made *me* nervous, because I didn't really want to get involved with those guys. But if Mikie said go, I'd most likely go.

Frankie had to help me out of bed the next morning. I tried and tried, but I hurt too much. I knew I'd be all right if I could get on my feet and start working the knots out, because that's the way it worked out yesterday and the day before. It was the getting to the feet that was the problem. So I rolled to one side, lay there taking deep breaths, then made the push. Nothing. I rolled to the other side, took the breaths, pushed, flailed one flipper like a beached you-know-what. Nothing.

I moaned. I lay there for a while making my mournful wail, resigned to spending the rest of that day flat out, as most of my good buddies passed by on their way to and from the bathroom.

"Hi."

"Hey there."

"How's it going?"

"Wimp."

"Blob."

"Good morning."

They all had something to say. I just waved back. Until Frankie came by. He was always the last one up.

"Jesus, why don't you quit, Elvin?" he suggested as he eased me to my feet. He had one hand on my back and one tugging me by the wrist. "Get yourself a new slot, for crying out loud. You gave it a shot."

"No. Don't . . . want . . . to... quit," I said, dividing my energy equally between speech and movement. "Like . . . it."

After one escorted lap around the barracks, Frank thought it safe to let me go. I was doing much better, and started in on my serious stretching. I got down on the floor and reached, with both hands, for my ankle. Today I nearly reached it. I wrapped my hands tightly around my calf and held the stretch. It burned my muscles to hold that for thirty seconds, but I did, smiling too, as I looked at the pen mark I'd made after yesterday's stretch. I was an inch closer today.

I did the same thing to the other leg, then looked up to see Frankie. He had the purple lotterylike sick-bay vouchers in his hand. "Here," he said. "Take a day off."

"I don't want a day off. I want to wrestle."

"Then wrestle tomorrow. You need a rehab day today." He pushed the vouchers at me.

I stared at them, then at him. "That's really nice, Frank. But I'm not seeing the nurse today."

He shoved them into my hand. "Then keep them for when you do need them."

"They're yours," I said.

"What am I gonna do, El, injure myself putting? Or drinking raspberry lime rickeys?"

I was incensed. "You guys get raspberry—"

"Somebody makes a run now and then to the Brigham's in town. Just keep the vouchers. To make me feel better."

"You could probably get five bucks apiece."

He nodded. "To make me feel better," he repeated.

Mikie was already munching a bran muffin when we walked into the dining hall. His two pints of milk were already empty, and he was starting on the grapefruit juice.

"Unsweetened? How can you drink that stuff?" I said,

sitting down with two miniature boxes of Rice Krispies, two blueberry muffins, and six strips of bacon.

"They really are great guys," Frank went on, as if we'd never left the table from last night's conversation.

People were picking up and moving on all around us. We were about the last ones in, what with Frankie's sleeping in and my palsy. So everybody was in a hurry, and it was one of those edgy mornings when nobody's interested in what the other guy wants to talk about.

"How old is this cereal?" I demanded to the room at large. "They're all duds. Hardly a crackle or pop in the box."

"These guys, they're the kind of guys who can really set you up, really improve your situation in the school," Frank said. "We'll be cool."

"Basketball Sector's okay," Mike answered a question nobody asked. "But some of the guys'll drive you crazy. I have this one guy, I don't know what it is, but he reminds me of you, Elvin."

I lifted my head from listening closely to the Rice Krispies. "Mikie, *no one* has *ever* been reminded of me by *any* basketball player. What's wrong with the guy?"

"I'm not sure. I keep giving him the ball in perfect position, and he keeps giving it right back to me. He could be really good, though. I'm working on him. I'm working on him hard."

"And they're a lot more fun than all these eighth graders around here," Frankie pushed. "Bet they have lots of real man-size fun planned for tonight. It'll be cool. *We'll* be cool."

"Do we really have to, though?" I asked, being uncool enough to ask such a thing. "Do we really *need* to be cool?"

He didn't puff up. He didn't joke. He didn't brag. "I do," Frankie said evenly.

Mikie stood up with his tray. "I have to go," he said. "My venue's all the way across the campus. And *I* have to walk." He winked at Frank.

"Oh, cut it out. They don't *send* the golf cart for me. We just get to drive it around on the course sometimes. Jeez, you guys."

"Go then," I said, pushing Frank along. "Get going. I have to sweep the floor here before I get to start."

"Oh ya," Frank said, seizing the opportunity. He hopped up and followed after Mikie, bending his ear about going tonight. It was funny, and somehow made me feel a little safer, that as big as he talked, Frankie still needed Mikie to okay it.

"Remember," Coach Wolfe stressed, "these exhibitions are for the purpose of getting you fellas some live-action experience, a chance to try out what you're learning, and to test your own readiness. They are *not* auditions for the school's wrestling team, and they are *not* some kind of accumulation of points in some imaginary standings. It is an educational exercise for all, and as such, I don't want anyone getting overzealous at this early stage of the game."

That speech, I realized, was for my benefit. Not that

my zeal was a threat to anyone. On the contrary, Coach was fearing for me as a *victim*. My man Axe did not appear to have any modulation control anywhere on his finely tuned thresher of a body, and his matches the first couple of days—against some pretty decent athletes—were wars. Wars he didn't lose.

My first two wrestling days, on the other hand . . . well, Coach put it generously when he said we were starting from scratch and building very slowly. The plan seemed to be to find my appropriate level of competition. For practice purposes all the "big 'uns," the junior heavyweights, heavyweights, and super heavyweights, did a lot of intermingling. Working my way down, I was thankfully allowed to go my first match against Eugene. A sport, a gentleman, a humanitarian, and a mentor, Eugene carried me through that whole match. He was good at making it look almost like a legitimate fight, taking the opportunity to show me a few new maneuvers along the way. He let me get to the second round before my inability to move him in any direction at all became just too obvious, and he finished me mercifully. He was even polite enough to whisper, "I'm going to have to pin you now," just before grinding me finally into the mat.

Eugene was the only super heavy, but there were two legitimate heavyweights. One was a real wrestler, so Coach bypassed him and matched me with the other guy, Bellows, a track-and-field washout who was cut for refusing to learn any kind of form in the shot put. Apparently he just kept heaving the thing like a lead softball and placing second or third anyway. Then he'd sit, a little Skoal Bandit pouch of tobacco under his lip, to shamelessly razz the opposition and spit brown streams across their line of vision. He was a jolly enough guy, in a menacing way, but he had pretty much the same approach to wrestling that he had to putting the shot. Form was an imposition; brute force was enough.

This much Bellows appreciated about the rules of wrestling: Get that sucker down, and flatten him there.

He achieved part A in ten seconds, meeting me headon, taking a hugging grip of both of my thighs, lifting me up and tackling me down. Hard. I felt the cartilage between my ribs crackle when we crashed together.

I wasn't giving up part B so quickly.

He didn't let go of my legs. He held and pushed, his feet digging in behind him as he drove me like a wheelbarrow farther into the floor. I twisted one way, flipped all the way over on my belly. With a vicious twist, he pulled me back. I leaned up, as if I were trying sit-ups, and he stood, still holding my legs, forcing my upper body to the mat again.

He let go of my legs when I wouldn't stop squirming side to side. He climbed up my body like a tree. Climbing horizontally up a felled tree. If he couldn't pin me with leverage, he was going to pin me with might. He grabbed the balls of both shoulders in his claws, and he squeezed. Squeezed and pushed.

I had no chance this way. I *never* had any chance of winning, but I never expected to. What was important, to me, was to not get pinned. I couldn't fight off this press, but I could writhe. I *let* him pin my left shoulder, giving it up so easily that all his weight fell to that side, and I lifted the other one. When he tried to compensate, I lifted the right.

"Predicament!" Coach called. "You're in a predicament, Elvin. Get out of it."

"Well, no shit," I grunted, as I strained to achieve zero improvement of the situation. I hadn't yet been told that a predicament in wrestling was when you were not quite pinned, but you might as well have been. And if you don't break out of it, they blow the whistle to stop the action.

Bellows was determined to pin me before that happened. With one hand still on each of my shoulders, he lowered his head and butted me in the chest.

The whistle blew. "Abusive move," Coach called.

"Ya," I concurred, gasping.

"No punishing moves," Coach told Bellows, slapping him on the shoulder. "That would cost you a warning in a real match. Two of 'em would cost you a point."

Bellows stuck out his hand and yanked me to my feet, even though I was quite happy where I was. "Okay, let's start over again," he said, bouncing anxiously.

"I think that's good for now, boys. Let the other guys have a crack," Coach said, and I almost hugged him.

"Nice job," Eugene whispered when I staggered back to the edge of the mat. "Way to hold that predicament."

I was still breathing hard, my ribs killing me with every heave, when I thanked him. I winced when Bellows came by and slapped my back.

But I liked it.

Axe, though. Axe was a different story entirely. Axe was the kind of guy who would slap your back only if you were standing on a cliff above a bay full of alligators. He was next on my dance card one rung down, at super middleweight.

Emphasis on the super. I never saw a kid so *hard* before. His arm muscles were dense and lashed with lumpy veins, his legs like two thick nautical ropes, and his bones—very dangerous—were practically filed to points on his elbows, cheeks, and temples. He had a face that never changed for anything, and looked like he didn't enjoy not one minute of whatever he was doing.

The only bright spots, as I could see them that morning, were the "no overzealous" speech and the soothing memory of "no punishing moves" from the day before. It would be all right, I thought, because I didn't have big aspirations here. I knew what was what. All I wanted was to hold my little bit of ground. Hold off on the pin. I could live in a predicament.

Yet when the match started, it all meant nothing.

Axe could wrestle. He did it all by the book, and nobody could stop him. When we met, the first thing he did was to slap away my outstretched hands, spin me around, and lock a grip on me from behind. He took his powerful right arm and threaded it up under my soft one. His hand held the arm from the inside of the elbow, and he yanked it almost behind me. Then his left hand came up and slapped onto my neck, and in one mighty, overwhelming swoop he flipped me to the floor.

I was nearly paralyzed. The move, and the hold that followed it up, were so efficient, so controlled, and it seemed to me so damn mean hearted, that I was immobile with dread. Axe now had my right arm pulled firmly back, and his left hand pressed so hard against the side of my head that the heel of his hand was leaving a bone bruise right behind my ear.

I looked out from under Axe's hand as he pressed my cheek to the floor. I could only see anything with the eye that was against the mat, the other being blocked by Axe's fingers. I felt like the helpless antelope I always saw on the nature show, the one that didn't get away, the one left staring big-eyed into the camera as the big cats swarm him and the rest of the herd escapes.

No punishing holds. My head hurt, my neck was twisted like a wrung towel. For one half of one half of a second my muscles thought there was a chance. Everything hurt ten times as much when I twitched. I was staring right into the faces on the sidelines, and they looked uncomfortable for me. I wished I could look away.

"That's enough, Coach," Eugene yelled out.

I hated that I was such an asshole as to think nobody could pin me.

"Predicament, Elvin," Coach yelled. "Break it."

At a certain point you always see the antelope stop kicking and lie back. I lay back.

An explosion. Axe released his grip, half lifted me, and slammed me flat on my back. He had caught me napping. I was pinned and croaked.

And pretty well broken.

I was still grieving over it as I sat in a folding chair in that same dining hall, munching popcorn and waiting for the movie to start at eight that night.

"That stuff is drenched in coconut oil," Mikie said, pointing at my large tub of popcorn. Just like the one he was eating.

"And butter," I added, staring at the blank screen. "And salt. I only wish they had some caramel to spray on it."

"So what's gone wrong, Elvin? You not an athlete anymore?"

I took a deep breath and was reminded. My ribs hurt. My shoulder hurt. My elbow felt as if I could bend it the wrong way if I wanted to. And even if I didn't want to, somebody would probably eventually do it for me.

"Come on, Mike, none of those jokes, okay?"

"Jesus," he said, quieting down and joining me in staring into the whiteness. "You sure are low tonight."

I was, and he was surprised by that. I was surprised by it myself. I guess I had managed to handle it a different way all the other times. So why was this different? was what I couldn't figure out at first.

Why was this defeat so different in a life that had

been so chockablock with little defeats?

I did know why it was different. It just took me a while to admit it. What was new here was that for the first time ever I was committed. I had declared myself, even if it was only *to* myself. I could joke off losses before because I never really wanted anything before. I never really *wanted* to be picked higher than last for touch football, I never really *wanted* to survive more than two minutes in dodgeball, I never really *wanted* to swim anything fancier than the dog paddle, so I could always say it was okay— because I wasn't really trying. But now I wanted something—a little something, but still something. I wanted it, I tried hard, and I could not do it.

I didn't want to win. All I wanted to know, all I needed, was this: Could I not get trashed? Could I do even that? Could I survive in that world that seemed to be coming toward me whether I liked it or not? Could I pick one thing, say *This is not going to happen to me*, and then make it not happen?

The answer today was No, and I had never felt so helpless in my whole helpless life.

"I hate it here, Mike," I said.

The credits started to roll on *Ernest Goes to Camp.*

"Could be worse," Mikie said, pointing at the screen.

"Even Ernest is more of a man than I am."

"Boy, you *are* low," he said.

Just then Frankie came up from behind. He had been sitting in back with the older guys. "So what's it going to be, guys?" he asked.

Mikie took the liberty of answering for both of us, which was usually fine. "Nah, Frank, I think I'm just going to stay and watch the movie with Ernest here."

"Mike," I whispered. "I want to go."

He turned to me, raised his eyebrows. "It's against the rules, you know."

"Ooo gee," I said, making an authentic dopey-Ernest face. "What do you think they'll do if they catch me? Send me home? Oh mercy, oh heavens, please, not that."

"Then I guess we're going." Mike shrugged.

"Yee-hah," Frank cheered quietly.

We rode together in Obie's ancient brown Chevy van—me, Mikie, Frankie, and two other counsellors, Okie and Odie. Obie drove. Bouncing around in the back of the van—which had no seats, just space and yellow shag carpeting top to bottom—I whispered to Frank how odd I thought his friends' names were.

"Bozo," he snarled into my ear, "those are just nicknames. Nobody has names like those. They're shortened. Obie, Okie, Odie. O'Brien, O'Connor, O'Donnell. Get it?"

"I get it, Frank, but I don't think that really shortens their names much. They save a syllable, big deal. Are they *that* busy?"

No one else could hear us over the music that was surging so hard through the cheap speakers that the songs were unidentifiable. There wasn't even a need for us to whisper. Despite this, Frank was mortified.

"We have to have a rule, Elvin. Whenever you feel like ridiculing people who could hurt us *bad*, you must run it by me before opening your mouth. You don't even appreciate nicknames, for god's sake."

"I'll type up all questions in advance," I said.

"That would be good, but we don't have time. Just don't embarrass me."

"What are you two talking about?" Mike asked, leaning in to hear.

"I'm embarrassing Frank."

"Well then, cut it out then, Elvin," Mike said. "We have to be on our best behavior or we won't be selected to hang out with Opie and Orgy and all the other guys."

"I knew, I knew this was a stupid idea. I knew you wouldn't appreciate this." Frank was very serious and frustrated. He moved away from us and sat up front with the counsellors.

"We could try to behave if it means that much to him," Mikie said, even though he was clearly acting up on Frank.

"I'll give it a shot," I said as the van skidded to a stop.

It was just like a camp. We piled out of the back to find a dozen more counsellors there, hanging around a campfire, telling dirty jokes, even cooking black hot dogs on sticks. The major difference was that they were also drinking beer, and nobody seemed to be in charge.

"Sure beats *Ernest Goes to Camp*, huh?" Frank said as Obie came by and handed each of us an icy-cold Coors as he made his rounds. I hesitated to take the beer until Frank gave me a pleading look.

"We'll see," Mikie said, accepting his too. "So far these guys aren't showing me anything."

Frank smiled, confident that we would soon see the beauty of it all. He opened his beer. "Onward to manhood, gents," he said, extending his bottle. We all three clicked our bottles together, though the "onward" thing was not all that clear.

Of all the boring things we'd done so far at camp, this was the most boring yet. Mike and I sat on a fallen tree and watched and listened, trying to somehow get it, to figure out what it was that was supposed to be so cool. I sipped my beer a few times, which I figured would help. It didn't, so I followed Mikie's lead by pouring it out gradually so it looked like we were drinking it.

This much I picked up: There was a connection between these guys and their penises and rock and roll.

"I call mine The Led Zeppelin," one of them crowed, yanking himself by the crotch. There were hoots from all over.

"I call mine Meat Loaf."

"Nothing. Forget it. You ready? Mine's Pink Floyd. Say hello to everybody, Floyd," the guy said, pulling down his elastic-waisted pants and shaking himself around.

"Shit, it *is* pink," Frankie blurted, which brought him a lot of attention.

"Ooohh, like it, Frankie boy?" the still-exposed counsellor said, marching Frank's way. Frank made the effort to laugh along with everyone as he backed up, but I could see a little worry on his face. Then somebody kneeled down behind him, the penis waver advanced, and *wham,* Frankie hit the deck just as Mikie yelled for him to look out.

They all sure found it funny. Frank tried harder than before to laugh harder than before. Okie or Odie or Oafie or somebody helped him and brushed him off while they all shared the good time. I looked at Mike, who shook his head and frowned.

Obie walked over to us and offered me an orphan hot dog that was so burned that it was maintaining a little flame. When I hesitated, he snarled at me.

Frankie took the hot dog, and received a loud pat on the back when he crunched away as if it was a raw carrot.

"Loosen up, you guys," Frank said as he washed it down with the beginnings of a second beer.

Mikie stood, looked at Frankie close up. "Honestly, Frankie, are you having fun here? I mean, do you *like* this?"

Frank looked over his shoulder at the counsellors drinking by the fire, punching each other and laughing. Then he looked back at Mike. "Ya, I really do," he said. Then something, the beer maybe, made his tone of voice change. "I wish you'd give it more of a chance, Mike. I mean, I know you're, like, perfect and so much friggin' smarter than me and all . . . but that doesn't mean being a piss all the time makes you better than everybody."

"I'm not a piss all the time," Mike said. "But maybe I am . . ." He caught himself, but he'd already said too much.

I found myself staring at Mikie now. It was okay for *me* to think he was better than us, but to hear him almost say it himself? He made it not true was what he did.

"What about you, Elvin?" Frank asked, waving Mikie off. More and more he seemed invested in this, like it was a party he himself was throwing, or like he was putting on a play and he wanted to know that everyone was enjoying it.

"Well, I took a pretty good beating today, Frank, so I have a headache. It wouldn't be fair for me to say."

He was disappointed. "Okay. I'm sorry. Why don't you take off. You can walk. It's not far."

Mikie got up. "That's probably a good idea," he said, looking down at me, waiting.

"Nah," I said. "I'm not in a big rush. I think I'll sit tight for a while."

Mikie's mouth dropped open. Frankie looked like he might hug me.

"Okay," Mikie said, shrugging. He turned and started down the hill, back to the road.

Frank took Mikie's spot on the log next to me. "Great," he said, nodding.

"I just didn't feel like leaving with him, like that."

"Well I'm glad, I'm glad, El. Can I get you a beer? Can I get you a dog? You don't have to have a burned one. I can get you a good one. I think you're gonna like these guys—I . . ."

"Frank," I interrupted, "I didn't want to leave with Mike, but I don't really feel like hanging around here either."

103

"Oh," he said quietly.

I stood, then Frank stood with me. He shrugged. He was coming along.

"You ain't leavin', are ya, dude?" Obie said, draping a big arm over his new protégé. "We're just gettin' started."

Frank gestured toward me. "Ya, well, my friends . . ."

"If the kids have to go to bed early, we understand. You ain't no kid, though, Frankie. No, you ain't no kid."

Frank turned back to me. "You mind? 'Cause if you mind . . ."

For just a flash I saw it—I thought I saw in his face that he maybe wanted me to say that I needed him to come back with me. But I couldn't know that for sure.

"I'm all set," I said. "Have a ball."

Obie was quick to jump in and send me on my way. "Ya just go through those trees there, stay on the path, and when ya hit the road take a right. It's only a mile."

As I headed into the trees, I heard huge, rough laughter from the whole crowd of them. I couldn't bring myself to look back at what it was about, though.

On the road back the moon was bright, like a single powerful streetlight following me home. Crickets and frogs and an owl sang me along, lulling me. Toads and opossums crossed the road like pedestrians at a crosswalk, ignoring me, and everything smelled like wet green.

The mile walk was approximately a half mile longer than I remembered ever walking before. I breathed harder. My ribs started hurting again. My elbow, my leg too. It made me remember today, and consider tomorrow. I didn't want to go through it anymore. Where had I put Frank's vouchers?

I was approaching the door to my Cluster and heard the ritual inside as Thor killed the lights: "Night, Knights," he said, sounding embarrassed like always. But it's part of the program, so he has to do it. "Night, Knights" came the first sarcastic chirp in reply. "Night, Knights," "Night, Knights," "Night, Knights," they all jumped in, eventually blending like a herd of giant crickets.

As I tiptoed into the Cluster, on into my bed, and hid behind my eyelids, somehow thinking I'd escaped notice, Thor's voice now wafted my way. "Be careful, Elvin." I opened my eyes to see him standing nearby. "Just be careful," he said, and walked back to his bed.

> Elvin Doe
> Elvin's Summer Cottage
> Midst of Other Lonely Boys
> Cluster Two, Massachusetts

Occupant
Elvin's Winter Home

Dear Birth Mother,

The entire compound is abuzz. Yes, that's right, it's almost time for Parents' Weekend. Can you think of anyone who might like to represent my family? Honestly, I've been wracking my brain and cannot come up with a soul who could fit the bill. There's a fellow named Duke who sleeps on the slab next to mine—sleeps, that is, when he's not sitting up rigid in the middle of the night *staring* at me while *I* try to sleep—and Duke has generously offered to help. Seems that Dukie has one mother and THREE fathers, and he'll be glad to lend me one. All I have to do is meet the man at the bus on Saturday, tell him I'm his son, and if I catch him at his drugs apex, he'll believe me.

But Duke says not to bet the farm on a medal in the three-legged race or the raw-egg toss, and under no circumstances am I allowed to let "Daddy" bob for apples.

Or maybe Save the Children could help me out somehow. Give Sally Struthers a call for me, would you? Oh, you're a dear.

Your biological son,
Oliver Twist

Chapter 7

Gonna flyyy nowww
(theme from *Rocky*).

wasn't up when Frankie came in, and he wasn't up when I went out. In fact, nobody in my Cluster was awake yet.

"Come on," Mikie whispered in my ear, "you need some work."

I opened my eyes. I was so thrilled and surprised to see him that I sat right up in bed, despite the morning pains. "Hey, bub, what's up? Am I at your house? Or are you at my house?"

He shook his head grimly when he saw my confusion. "Sorry. Still at camp."

"Ugh," I said, and threw myself back down on the bed. He pulled me back up to sitting position.

"Come on, Elvin, it's a great morning. I'm taking you running."

He had to cover my mouth when I laughed out loud.

"I'm serious, El. It's going to make you feel better. This whole stupid thing will work out better if you just get yourself in a little bit of shape. We'll start slow. There's a nice hiking trail we can use that I found walking around during Reflective Period."

I looked at him. He wore shorts, a tank top, and a determined expression.

"You're serious."

"Very."

"I might die, you know."

"You might."

"That'll teach my mother. Let me get my big red shorts on."

We tiptoed out, backtracking to check out Frank before we left. He was spread out on his bed, limbs splayed like a starfish. He had no sheet covering him and he looked all sticky, lying on his back in his underwear like you do when it's a rotten hot summer night. Even though last night was just a rotten cool summer night.

Just outside the door, Mikie did his warm-up stretching silently. Grab the toe with the hand behind the back and bend way over forward. Touch the toes and hold it. Spread those feet . . . how far apart? "Oww, stop it, stop that," I said. He laughed and finished, pulling one knee at a time to his chest.

"You're up," he said, pointing at my legs.

"I'm out," I said.

"You're in."

He manhandled me. Slapped my legs, pulled one foot as far as he could away from the other, slapping, pushing, slapping, like the elephant trainer in the circus, until he'd squeezed me as much as he could.

"Now, Elvin, taking your right hand, I want you to reach over your head, stretch your top half to the left, and reach for the ground, as if you were making an arc over your whole body with your right hand trying to get to your left foot."

"I will *not*," I said indignantly.

He knew he had me sort of frozen there, which is why he knew he could grab my hand and forcibly *pull* me over into the unnatural position he wanted.

"Ow, Mikie, Jesus, Mikie, hell, Mikie, Jesus, Mikie," I squealed.

He started laughing, then pulled me the other way. "If you want to avoid injuries, El, you have to prepare yourself."

"I should be preparing myself for breakfast right about now."

"Ya, well I don't think it would hurt for you to skip breakfast this morning, either. Just have a piece of fruit and some juice."

"Well, I guess I should do what you tell me," I said, poking him, "since you're so much *better* than the rest of us."

"I never said that," he said, pulling me up by the

armpits so that my feet could finally get back together again. Just as I sighed, he put both hands on my back and bent me over.

"Well, you said *most* of it."

"No, I thought about it later, and I decided that you guys were wrong; I did not say it."

"Gee, even when you're by yourself you're superior, huh?"

"We're not here for me—"

"No, we never are. You're so *good*, Mikie. I'm not worthy."

"Okay, you win. I'm better than everybody. Now touch those toes and we're out of here, Elvin."

I hung there, touched halfway down my shins, then straightened up. "We're out of here," I said, leaning my face into his.

He punched me in the belly, but not hard, then bolted.

"How long did you stay?" he asked as we set out on the road.

"I left right after you."

"Good. So what time did *he* come in?"

"I don't know, Dad. I was asleep."

"Stay awake next time. I want to know."

"I'll see what I can do. Say, what's the rope for?" Mike had a rope, like a clothesline, coiled diagonally around his body.

"Thought we might try some rock climbing, if a good spot presents itself." He was running ahead with his back to me, so I couldn't see if he was grinning, but he had to be. He had to be trying to get a rise out of me, because he couldn't be serious. The only thing to do when he's like that is to ignore him, so I did.

It wasn't so bad, those first few yards. Mike was right, it was a beautiful morning, so beautiful that for a while my body didn't even occur to me. Some strange birds made *whoo-ti-whoo* and *keekle-dee-gee* songs, sounding like they were perched right on our ears. There was a little dewy water hanging everywhere, cool and sweet. The *crunch-crunch* of sticks and pine needles under our feet somehow made me feel it more, that we were accomplishing something before breakfast.

"Don't bounce so much," he said, running backward to go as slowly as me.

"Sorry, but it's just impossible for me to make this much movement without bouncing at least a little."

"I don't mean *jiggling*—I know you can't help that. I mean bouncing. Up and down. You're doing more vertical moving than horizontal."

I nodded, concentrating on my motion instead of talking. Because now, a quarter mile into it, I was starting to *feel* it. So I reduced the bounce. My feet skimmed the surface of the road. I was still slow, but I was more efficient.

"Good, there you go. Doesn't that feel better?" he said as he went back to running forward.

"Unh," I answered.

By the half-mile mark the thrill was gone. I was spewing sweat like the sprinkler system down on Frankie's golf course. I kept chugging, though, on through where the road turned to trail, and where the trail turned to path. The terrain also turned, from flat to rolling to just plain *up*. I was keeping Mikie in sight up ahead, but he was getting smaller.

I crawled along, putting as much pump into breathing as I was into advancing. The trees still passed by me on both sides, but more slowly now. Then the whole scene stalled, seemed to go nowhere for the longest time, as if I was running on a treadmill and not getting anywhere.

But through the fog of my heat vapors, Mikie actually was getting bigger. He wasn't losing me. The gap was closing. Something must have been working right.

"You okay?" he asked, putting his hand on my stomach to steady me.

"I am," I said, and I did feel better with him nearer.

"You want to quit?"

"I don't want to quit. Soon, I will. But not yet."

Mike smiled a firm sort of proud Marines smile. Next thing I knew, there was a tug at my middle. I looked down to see him tying the rope around my waist. He'd already looped it around himself, and we were lashed together.

"When you want to stop for good," he said, "just fall down. I'll get the message."

And off he went. I staggered to get a little momentum before the fifty feet of rope between us pulled taut, but it did as soon as I moved. He jerked me ahead at first, but I got my balance. Mike slowed his pace a bit—okay, he slowed it a ton. But I kept with him. Then, being so close now, watching his correct form, listening to him—

"Concentrate on your breathing, make it smooth," he kept saying—I worked up an imitation of what he did. My right hand went forward when my left leg went forward. My left hand went back when my right leg went back. I breathed rapidly but regularly, one breath in, then one out, on each footfall. I never found myself with both hands at my sides at the same time, as I had at the bottom of the hill.

After several minutes I picked up a few steps, and the tension on the rope slackened. "There you go, Elvin, how you doing?" Mike said while looking back over his shoulder. I nodded, and I think managed something like a smile.

So he increased the pace. I had been sure that we had already maxed me out, but when I felt the rope tug at me from the middle, I shortened my stride, started dropping my feet a quarter step quicker. I kept up. He pulled me just enough and not too much, so that I could do what he was making me do. The pace he already figured I could do.

"All right there, El? All right?" he called once more, his words choppier now, his voice much breathier.

". . . right," I croaked.

". . . 'Most there," he said, and made one more quick jump up in the pace. The hill was cresting; I could feel it lessen. Still I nearly fell this time, even put my hands out in front of me before righting myself. I reached the new pace, held it for a minute of panting, wobbling, careening, before we reached the end and staggered into camp.

It was just short of a mile, mostly uphill, and it took us just under half an hour to do it. I fell flat on my face and rubbed it back and forth in the dew, then rested there happily on my forehead. In another minute I looked up to find Mikie sitting on a rock, sweating and panting almost as hard as I was, his head between his knees.

It was only then that it occurred to me, because I was thinking about me like I always do. Mikie *towed* me up that hill. And I outweighed him by twenty-five pounds.

After a struggle, I got to my feet. He still had his head down when I got to him.

"You going to barf?" I asked.

"Noooo," he drawled, then stood up too quickly, to prove it. I saw him waver for a second; then he was all right. Then he wasn't again. "Jesus," he said, and walked past me.

The place we'd landed was the party place where we'd been with Frankie and all his new buddies the night before. There were a lot of smashed bottles around, making the ground like a jagged gravel driveway. At the far end of the campfire circle three trees were covered, their trunks plastered with pages and pages from nudie magazines. But not the magazines I knew of, with round-faced blond ladies who could just be the local Dairy Queen queen if it wasn't for the enormous gold breasts and the eight miles of hair they could pull down their backs and thread between their legs. No, these magazines here had *lots* of people in the pictures, being all kinds of busy in ways I had never even thought of in the longest sleepless summer night. And the pictures were angrier than the ones I remembered from *Playboy.*

There was a stench of burned rubber still hanging there in the middle of the dead campfire, and it wasn't too hard for Mikie and me to guess whose size-ten basketball shoes were sitting there charred and black in the ashes.

Nice shoes too, they were, before. Frank's stuff was always nice. It was important to him, more important than to anyone else I knew, to have nice things. And to look good. Must have hurt like sticking his actual feet in that fire, to burn his shoes. I wondered if he laughed that one off too.

Mike shook his head and walked, two and three and four times circling the ring of stones framing the fire pit. "They'll probably stop soon, don't you think?" he asked, as if I knew. "They'll just treat him jerky for a little while, then that'll be his initiation, then he can just be in their dopey club, right?"

I circled with him once, the rope still tethering us, but then I sat down to get something back in my legs. I started to answer, then looked at Mike looking up into the sky. I realized he wasn't asking me the question, he was asking himself.

"It stinks here," I said.

"Ya, it really stinks," he repeated.

"We should be getting back," I said, wanting to get him away from what was only going to piss him off. "And," I added brightly, standing and stretching a little, "since you did all that work on the way up, this one's on me. Down is my specialty, you know."

"What?" he said, but we didn't have time for that. I

took off, barreling out of that camp and assaulting the downside of that trail like there was a bear on my back. Mike made hysterical cackling noises, trying to stay up through the first couple hundred yards when I was so possessed that I barely kept my feet myself. The breeze was back in my face; gravity was now, for a change, my friend; and though I was weak in the knees and afraid of what every new step was going to bring, I kept on wheeling madly, watching my legs spin like the paddles of a big steamboat.

I bounced off a soft bending birch tree but kept going. I stepped ankle deep into a brook I hadn't found the first time. I heard myself wheeze, but it was half from laughing, so instead of slowing, which my body was now screaming at me to do, I pressed. I saw the bottom of the hill coming up, and I pressed harder.

Into the ground was where I pressed. Just as the ride was about to flatten out, my legs just quit. My hands were too slow to get out in front when my leg refused to extend that one more time, and I hit the earth facefirst. All my weight, and gravity, and Mikie, who I didn't realize was right up my back, came slamming down on top of me as I hit, flipped, flopped heels over head, finally landing on my back in the path. Mike bounced off me and caromed off the slope of the road, momentarily out of view. All I could see when I turned my head that way was the rope, still connecting us, as it dipped down and over.

He was laughing spastically as he climbed the rope, using me as an anchor. I almost choked myself as I joined him, laughing as I lay on my back removing a big lump of pine bark from my cheek and pine needles from my gums.

"Do you think you can you get up?" he asked, though he didn't look too concerned about it.

"Do I want to is the question," I answered. But I did, both. I wanted to, and I got up, slowly. "Maybe we should walk it in from here, huh, Mike?"

He agreed, and we took it slow for the rest of the way, walking still tied up along the road.

People were just starting to roll out in my Cluster when I slogged through, showered, and dressed my mole quickly, then left again. Frankie was not yet up.

Taking Mikie's advice, I grabbed an apple, a nectarine, and a carton of cran-grape juice and beat it out of the dining hall before I went after real food. They had those coffee crumb cakes this morning, the kind in the two-packs with the little balls of brown whatever-it-is on top that make me insane. I had to run.

I stopped running, of course, as soon as possible. On the porch of the dining hall. From there, on top of everything, I could scan, and pick a spot far away from the maddening food smells inside. There, at the far corner of the valley in the middle of the complex, was the loneliest building in the place. The library.

"Go for it," I thought. Why not find something on wrestling? There were books on everything else, so maybe I could uncover a few tricks that could give me an advantage. It was a long shot, but I needed something.

Besides, I was sure nobody else in wrestling was reading his way to the top.

It was fun to walk into the dark empty library. The lights were off, the sun barely seeped in, dust had gathered on all the mahogany paneling. And it was even cool. The place hadn't been warmed by the heat of a single body since the summer started. It was a temptation to let loose a scream, the stillness was so inviting, and the place was so totally mine.

I did not, as I have always not, resist the temptation.

I hid in a stack of books as I waited for my echo to die and the No Excessive Pleasure Police to come and haul me off. But since the Knights could probably hear gunplay and not respond if it was only the library getting shot up, I was safe.

One of the reasons nobody used the place, I realized, was that it was ninety percent filled with religion books. Old, old religion books. Also a smattering of psychology books, dealing mostly with religion. They had a small science section that was so exciting, it made me lonely for the religion books; a Great Works of Literature section all full of English textbooks—*that* kind of great literature—and a Latin section. Art, music, and theater were lumped together on a three-shelf stack, on top of which rested the world's first copying machine.

And then there was the sports section.

If any of the guys came here looking for *Rare Air*, by Michael Jordan, I believe they would have been put on a waiting list of about seven thousand years. The Greatest

Stars of Today series of baseball books included a volume on Duke Snider. There was a book on Wimbledon with pictures of women players who wore longer skirts than the nuns did in my old school.

Then there was the Creative Sports Series of the Physical Fitness Program published by the Creative Educational Society of Mankato, Minnesota. This series must have been the core of the seminary's stellar and rigorous athletic program, because they had all the books in the series, all nineteen of them, from *Archery* to *Badminton* to *Table Tennis* to *Waterskiing*. All the big ones.

And right there, beaming out at me from position fourteen, its uncracked plain red spine gleaming, was *Wrestling*.

I sat down with it and cozied up with my new main man. Rummy Macias, Wrestling Coach, Mankato State College, Mankato, Minnesota.

First I was hooked on the name. If the guy's name was Rummy, must he not be one tough mother? Then he had the endorsements in the front of the book, from the wrestling coaches at both Oklahoma State and Iowa State Universities. *Universities*. One of the coaches even called Rummy the "Mr. Wrestling" of the state of Minnesota. I had heard of those colleges. Much tougher than this small-time high school Knights stuff. I could learn something that would get me there, beyond my competition, even if Rummy and his black-and-white crew cut were a tiny bit, well, dated.

And one of the demonstrator wrestlers in the pictures

had *the* hairiest arms and back I'd ever seen. I was checking this book *out*. I signed myself a card and stamped it before leaving.

I passed Mikie and a tired-looking Frank on my way back through the dining-hall door.

"Morning, Buck," I said to Frankie. I was feeling the power and improvement already as I carried the book, all the great grappling secrets tucked under my arm—though not yet tucked into my head.

He looked at me through droopy lids. "Missed a fun time, boy."

"I'm an athlete, Francis. I need to be in bed early."

Frankie just laughed at me. Mike took the book from me and checked it out. "Good," he said. "You're going to apply yourself."

I nodded forcefully, and he did the same in return. I took my book and marched inside.

All I had time for before getting to business was a quick shot of inspiration from Rummy. I cracked the book open to the introduction and was rewarded immediately.

It is normal for every boy to want to wrestle. From early childhood one of his greatest pleasures is a good tussle. It is the coaches' responsibility to direct and train this desire for satisfying activity in such a way that it will culminate in superior fitness.

I felt like such an animal. It surged in me, this beastly thing, this desire for satisfying activity. I had that desire.

I wanted a good tussle. Right now.

I came thumping out of the dressing kitchen anxious to get to work. Eugene was already giving a mighty lesson to the unteachable Bellows. I went directly to the weight chart to see who was on the menu today. I was free-falling now, tumbling down through the weight divisions, as the coach searched for somebody I might be competitive with.

Today I drew Victor the welterweight, a mere thirty pounds below me. Too bad for Victor—it wasn't his fault. The fall would stop with him, and I then I'd reverse field to take my revenge on those who had wronged me earlier. Like in *Carrie*.

Victor and I shook hands before the match. Good grip there, Vic. Vic was one of those confirmed wrestlers.

Within five seconds, he had a lock on my leg and was working feverishly to lift me off balance. I pushed down on his shoulders; he jerked me back up. Finally, I fooled him. As soon as I had him pushed halfway down again, I dropped.

Victor went flat as a spatula. I spread myself as wide and bulky dead as possible, praying he couldn't get me off. He pushed, lifted himself off the floor like a push-up with me on top. I was lost. He actually crawled several steps with me up there helplessly along for the ride like a parade float, bringing a few laughs. I honestly didn't know what to do. Anything I'd ever done before, that was all just weight. I dropped on a guy, I grabbed, pulled, rolled on him. But I hadn't really done one bona-fide

121

wrestling maneuver in the five days I'd been in wrestling. It was time to quit that.

I reached down and put a lock on Victor's arm just as he was about to roll me. As hard as I could, I yanked, tripping him.

Just like something that would happen to me, Victor fell straight over, onto his face. On his back I rode him into the floor. One of his shoulders was down, and it was staying down, dammit, as I put everything I had into the effort of keeping my welterweight stuck to the floor in whatever position he was in when I got him there. I wouldn't even consider trying to turn him over and get a full pin. I was a lot of things, but I was not stupid. And I wasn't giving this back. He pushed, thrashed, reached up behind him with his good hand to try and get some piece of some part of me, but I had that one shoulder nailed, the arm tucked under him.

"Predicament," Coach called out, and I almost started trying to kick out until I remembered I was the *top* guy.

The whistle blew, and Coach came out. Eugene stopped what he was doing and came too. I rolled off Victor and punched the mat with both fists, I was so charged.

When Victor got up, Coach had to pull him away, because he couldn't wait to get back to round two. Coach had to jam the white towel up under Victor's nose, then pull it out to show him the blood hosing out. He'd landed squarely on the nose, but it didn't seem to bother him much. He was tough, and must have landed on that nose plenty of times before, only not with two and a half times his weight behind it.

"You did all right," Eugene said as Victor walked himself off to the nurse's station with his nose bundled. "You held him; that's the job. Good." He helped me to my feet, and I wobbled. The adrenaline splashing through me now was making me woozier than the morning run up the mountain had.

"That was—it was a good move, Elvin," Coach Wolfe said. "It only kinda makes me wish we coulda seen what woulda happened in round two and three."

I didn't want to think about that. I wished he hadn't said it. But he was right to. It was only one move, and a half-belly-flop move at that. Victor was good. Victor knew how to do stuff, and given more time, he would have figured me out. I had to know more.

"Can I go some more, Coach?" I asked.

"That's the spirit, son," he answered brightly. Coach motioned for the other welterweight to come on over, and back we were.

This one, Lute, was not as strong as Victor, but he was less inclined to stay still for me. He first faked the same leg grab Vic used; then when I went for it, he scooted around behind me. Also just like Victor, Lute put a hold on me that people seemed to find funny.

Why do people think it's so funny when a fat kid tries hard?

He wrapped his arms around my middle and

123

squeezed, as if he was trying to get a chicken wing out of my throat. I walked, dragging him, then tried awkwardly to reach from one side and then the other around my back. I could not get him and he would not let go. I bent way forward to try and flip him over, but he dug in.

For a moment I stood motionless and clueless. I suddenly got so embarrassed, with Lute squeezing me from behind and me helpless to stop him, that I almost just said, "Okay, stop. That's it, just get off and leave me alone."

But I didn't have to. Even that would have been better than what did happen.

Quick as a snake, and suddenly strong in just the same way, Lute hopped up and coiled his legs up around my thighs and his arms in around my arms. He leaned backward, catching me by complete surprise, and pulled.

We both went over backward, slamming to the floor. But he wouldn't let me stop moving. By inching his body down, pulling my top and kicking my bottom at the same time, Lute pulled me down, rolled me up onto my back, then all the way up onto my shoulders. In one of the most painful, precarious moments of my life, he had me with my legs up in the air, my head bent sideways, all my weight resting on my neck. Lute was still draped over me, only now he had me all curled in and staring straight at my own navel. And with both shoulders welded to the floor.

Coach Wolfe blew the whistle as soon as Lute had the position locked. Then he let me go and I fell in a heap.

"No," I insisted. "I don't want to go to the nurse. I'm fine." I couldn't even turn my head to face the coach without shifting my whole body.

"Just have it looked at—you shouldn't mess with vertebrae." He motioned for Eugene to take me out. "Everybody knows now you're a gamer, Elvin. Nobody's going to think any less."

"I don't want to be a gamer," I thought as I went meekly. "I want to be good at this."

When I got to the bay, Victor was just pushing the ice away, saying, "Enough," to the nurse's assistant.

"Good move back there, man," he commended me as they laid me down in his old spot. "So what happened, you put a move on yourself this time?"

"You could say that," I said.

"Well, come back soon," Victor said as he headed back to the trenches, " 'cause I can't wait to *kick your ass*." He laughed, because that was his idea of fun. Victor loved his work.

Maybe it was the vicious pinning I took from Lute. Or maybe it was fighting two real matches in one day. Or maybe it was the no real breakfast, or the early run. Probably it was all of it, and all of it being so far from any way I'd ever been before. Whatever the reason, when the nurse gave me two anti-inflammatories and told me I had to lie there for a while, I didn't mind. Even though I really didn't want to be there. The ward was half empty by this stage in the game; all the real needies were out of vouchers by now and slogging through the Sectors half dismembered. So it was quiet. And cool. And undemanding of me.

I fell asleep, and I stayed asleep until they figured they should wake me for Nightmeal.

When I walked all bleary back into the dining hall, it was a dining hall again. It was beginning to feel like a weird funny movie where I just kept walking back and forth between two or three locations, I'd get mugged, and while I was out somebody'd quickly switch around all the decor to drive me insane until I didn't know who or where I was.

It was working beautifully.

I waved to the Indian on the Massachusetts flag as I passed under. He waved back.

"What are you doing with my book?" I said as I walked up to Mikie at our table. "Give me that." I swiped it back.

He shrugged. "It was here on the table when I got here. It must have been in here since you brought it this morning. I think it's a good idea, Elvin, to study up, but keep it in perspective."

"Meaning what?"

"Meaning it's kind of an old book. And meaning no book is going to make you great overnight. You may have to consider that you might never be great at this. Or that maybe it'll take a fair amount of time."

"I know that," I said snottily, turning my head—that is, my head and neck and shoulders and upper back as one rigid unit—for emphasis.

"What happened to your neck?"

"Jeez, Mikie, can't we talk about something else for a change? What is it with you, it's always wrestling, wrestling, wrestling, wrestling lately."

He got the picture. "Okay, El, new subject. Your mother coming this weekend?"

"I won one today."

"Excuse me?"

"I won a match. Beat the bejesus out of one very tough welterweight."

Mike extended his hand across the table and shook mine. "Hell, El, awesome. You pin him?"

"Nah." I took a big satisfied bite of dry French bread from a basket on the table. My mouth filled to capacity with chalky bread, so Mikie had to wait. Finally I said, "Nah. Fell on him. Bloodied his nose up pretty good, though."

"Well there you go. It's a start."

"Yup. A finish too. The next little welterweight spun me on my head like a figure skater and put *me* in sick bay."

Mike stared at me deadpan. "El, there may be guys who want to be here more than you do—"

"Ya, like maybe three *hundred* of them—"

"But there sure isn't anybody getting more bang for the buck than you."

"Except me," Frankie said, slipping in beside Mike.

"You look better than this morning," I said.

"You don't," Frankie answered. "But we can fix that.

You guys want another chance tonight? The O's—that's what we call Obie and Okie and all those guys—the O's kind of think you two are wimps, but I told them you're cool and you should have another chance."

"Spare me," Mike said.

"Ya, spare me too," I said.

"Come on, guys," Frank said. "Tonight's movie night. *Real* movie night. Not like *Ernest Goes to Camp* chump stuff. More like *Felicia Goes to Camp*. It's going to be *wild*, and you're invited."

"Take a night off, why don't you, Frank," Mike snapped.

"No way. This is the night. We have the flicks. We borrowed a projector and a screen and a generator from the seminary—they were very generous about it. Once-in-a-lifetime stuff."

"This sounds dangerous, Frank," I said, "taking stuff from the school."

"Don't be so serious, Elvin. This is the kind of stuff guys do together. This is what that brochure of yours was talking about, bonding stuff. It's going to be *hot*."

"Franko," Mikie said, "let's make you a deal. Stick around camp for one night, and we promise Elvin and me will bond with you. Won't we, El?"

"Well, ah, what exactly is involved with that?" I asked. "Sounds a little complicated to me. I've got a lot on my plate as it is, and I'm not sure I could manage . . ."

"We'll listen to your stories," Mike encouraged Frank further. "The nun story and the Avon lady story and the crossing-guard story like we never heard them before. We'll boost a ton of Cokes and SuzyQ's from the dining hall and pound them down until we're so mental we can't sleep all night and we can't stop talking."

"Listen to him, Franko," I leaped in. "He's making a lot of sense here."

He was listening, with a dopey little-boy smile coming across him that made him look younger, less smarty-pants. Happier.

"We'll even tell you some stories about you that you don't even know. The ones that we make up to tell the girls in the school yard."

Frankie looked hooked. "Like when it was just us," he said, kind of dreamy, "and everybody else was kind of outside."

"Right," Mikie and I chirped together.

There was a long pause. I felt the long day gaining on me and popped some more bread to fight the oncoming woozies of fatigue.

"Okay," Frank said easily. "To tell the truth, I could use a night off from—"

"From being hazed?" Mike snipped.

"I'm not being hazed—that's so totally wrong. I'm being . . . ceremoniously welcomed."

"Jeez," I said, pulling back. "That sounds like it would hurt even *more*."

"Tell me something, Franko," Mike asked. "You really like those guys? Honest?"

Frank dragged out the word way too long to actually

mean it. "Ahhyyyya, y-ya I like them. They're cool. They're, y'know, I'm learning to like them."

"I see," Mikie said. "Why bother, if you have to learn to like them?"

"Okay, never mind. You'll see, later on. You'll thank me for breaking us in."

"Okay," Mikie said, "I'll see."

Frank got up from the table. "All right, I just have to run ahead and tell them I'm out for tonight. Then I'll meet you guys back here. Elvin, save me some SuzyQ's."

"I'll try my best," I said, "but you better hurry."

We took our sweet time with dinner, dragging it out until we were the last ones eating. Then when the two guys who were that night's sweepers started cleaning up, Mikie and I went over and volunteered to relieve them, to get rid of the final witnesses.

They were pretty grateful. And I didn't even mind the extra work, since I'd been doing it every morning after Mornmeal and before wrestling. I was starting to take a strange, satisfying pleasure in my skill with the big industrial broom. Though I didn't tell anyone about it.

When we were done sweeping, we slipped into the kitchen. We opened the big red-and-white floor cooler and pulled out fifteen cans of Coke, stuffing them into brown shopping bags. Then we went to the stack of metal cage shelves, scanning the dessert possibilities.

"How can they have no more SuzyQ's?" I barked. "What kind of a savage joint is this anyway?"

"Shaddup," Mikie said. "You want to get caught?

Look, at least they have Sno Balls."

"Sno Balls? The pink Sno Balls? In place of *SuzyQ's*? Jeez, I'm embarrassed to be seen stealing food with you."

"Elvin, Sno Balls *are* SuzyQ's, only with hats on."

"And I thought you were smart. And I thought you had taste. Sometimes, the things you say—"

While I was ranting, Mikie had ripped the packaging off a pair of Sno Balls. Then he jammed one in my gaping mouth. I bit, chewed, swirled it around in there.

I started tossing Sno Balls into the bags.

"But they are not the same as SuzyQ's," I said. "That rubbery skin makes it a whole different ball game. So you were not right."

We left our haul just inside the doors and went out on the porch to wait for Frankie with three cold Cokes.

"Taking him a long time," I observed.

"Uh-huh," Mike answered.

"Is he not coming, do you think?"

"No. He wouldn't not come. He can be jerky, but he's always there, you know?"

"Ya. I know."

We'd just about finished the first Cokes when we saw the van, the O'Van, angling across the compound. It wound around the road, hopped the rounded asphalt curb, and came heading our way over the grass. When it skidded to a stop about twenty feet away from us, Frankie was sitting sheepishly in the shotgun seat, on the side closer to us. Obie was driving. There was a lot of banging around and raunchy laughing in back.

"We're really sorry, boys," Obie said, leaning across Frankie to yell to us. "I know you wanted him, but we just couldn't spare him tonight. But he did insist on coming back to tell you himself."

Frankie hung his head out the window. Obie, behind him, couldn't see Frank's face. "Maybe tomorrow night," Frank said. "Okay? I just can't tonight."

He had an apology on his face that just didn't come out of his mouth.

Mikie and I simply nodded, as if there was any choice. Obie took that as a signal to hit the gas and peel away.

When they were good and gone, I went inside and got two more Cokes and two packs of Sno Balls. Then Mikie and I sat ourselves down on the porch. I told Mikie the story about Frank and the crossing guard. He told me the one about Frank and the school committeewoman. We got pretty sugared up and stupid after a while and toasted Frankie and laughed a lot at all the stories. But we didn't laugh as much as we would have. We didn't laugh as much as we had before.

We put most of the stuff back in the kitchen before we headed back to the Clusters.

"See," I said just before we split up, "I told you Sno Balls wouldn't be the same as SuzyQ's."

Since I'd slept all day, then gotten wired up with Mikie, sleeping all night was sort of a problem. Long after all the "Night, Knights," and after the hard-core snorers kicked in, even after Duke stopped staring at me, finally keeled over on his side, and passed out, I was still awake. I lay in bed with the long red flashlight Thor had lent me, poring over the words of Rummy Macias.

I had started out a little ambitiously, zooming from the table of contents right to page 114 and the heading "Opponent on His Knees." It just sounded so good. Like: Read this page and your life will all come together before morning.

Unfortunately, page 114 didn't tell me how to get an opponent to his knees, only what to do with him once I'd gotten him there. Clearly, Rummy and I were ahead of ourselves here.

The next most exciting thing to me was the Whizzer Series of moves, beginning on page 89. Before I went to it, I closed the book and just stared at the darkened ceiling, playing it in my head. The Whizzer Series. Whizz. Whizz kid. Whizz-bang Bishop. I Whizz. See that Bishop kid out there, sure is a goddamn Whizzer, ain't he? Whizzzzzz.

I liked it. I loved it, to tell the entire truth. I felt lighter already. I'd wear silver shoes.

I refused to open the book to page 89 and investigate the Whizzer Series any further. I would not pollute my imagination with reality.

The Trip Series, page 85, caught my eye. They allow tripping? If they allowed tripping, I reasoned, then this could certainly be an area I could specialize in. So I read.

As it turned out, Rummy's tripping was a little more complicated than sticking out your foot when the other guy runs by. I read the whole section, but it didn't turn out to be the beacon I had hoped for. These moves were as complicated as any of the others, involving hands, feet, balance, strength, and all that hooey. I got more discouraged.

I still couldn't sleep, and I couldn't read anymore. I clicked off the flashlight, pulled on some clothes in the dark, and slipped outside.

I followed the route Mikie had showed me that morning. It was dark now, but the moon was strong again and the paths were fairly smooth. And halfway there, I had the grunts and slurs of the O's to guide me.

I stepped very lightly as I approached the edge of their camp. The fire was almost dead, but they weren't gathered around that anyway. They sat in tiers, on rocks and logs and sometimes on each other, like a miniature primitive temple as they prayed to the grainy silver glow on the screen. The *grrr* of the generator and the *tickey-tick* of the reels were all the soundtrack I could hear. Down in front center, almost like he was forced to stay in that spot, was Frankie. He was as big as half of them there, but kneeling and slumped, he looked very small.

The next flick started without fanfare. And as soon as it did, I was transfixed. I froze, puck-eyed, from the first frame.

It was a thing called *Barnyard Hijinks*, in which a woman did . . . things—there can't be words, actual dictionary words with pronunciations and definitions, to label some of these acts. With animals. I didn't recognize the backgrounds in the film, other than that it was a farm, but wherever this took place had to be a country with no laws. This one lady, and her lovely assistant, had several farm beasts working harder than any creature has labored since the invention of the mechanical tractor. I was sure there would have to be some special-effects trickery going on with some of those stunts, except the picture seemed to be made on somebody's grandfather's 16-millimeter hand crank.

When it got to be too much to bear, I turned from the screen back to Frankie. I noticed that two of the bigger guys flanked him, like guards. When Frank looked away from the screen, one of them pushed his face back into viewing position. The other grabbed his wrist and coaxed Frankie's beer bottle back up to his lips. As he drank, somebody slapped him hard on the back. The movie was gross, but what Frankie was putting up with was a lot harder to look at.

I slithered back down the hill, feeling weak and a little sick in the belly. With all the roars of laughter, nobody heard me crunching through the woods. I slogged back to camp with the noise gradually shrinking away behind me.

I lay in bed more sleepless than before until, about an hour and a half later, Frankie came trudging through.

"So, how were the movies?" I whispered as he passed my bed.

He stopped. "All right," he said. "A couple of them were great. A couple of them I didn't like so much." He said it, especially the last part, with a heavy tired voice. He forced a smile and went on to bed.

Big Mama Bishop,

Not *sure*? What do you mean, "Not sure"? You're *not sure* if you can make it this weekend? No, Mother, I will *not* sit tight until you hear back whether Aunt Mamie can go with you to Presque Isle for the weekend. I don't care what you say, I did so tell you it was *this* weekend. Just tell Aunt Mamie I'm sure Presque Isle has enough lonely police officers and lobster trappers to tide her over for the two days before you can get there.

Don't toy with me, Mother. I'm not the frail lumpen lad you shoehorned onto that yellow bus a mere forty days and forty nights ago. I'm mean now, like, *Lord of the Flies* mean, because of what you did to me, so you better not fool around. Everybody here is afraid of me.

And this is put-up-or-shut-up time around here. This is when you have to produce hard evidence that you have actual parents and that you weren't just left here on the grounds when the circus moved on to Providence. If your family does not show up, you're put into a group informally known as "The Unloved," who, legend has it, roam around like a pack of wild dingoes all weekend doing unspeakable things to themselves and others.

And I could well do it. Take me seriously, Mother. I'm learning new ruffian stuff every day. I have a book.

Elvin "Rummy Junior" Bishop

PART 3

WEEK THREE

Chapter 8

Oh yes, my *other* family.

t's not really even a weekend anyhow. In fact, it's not even twenty-four hours. The parents arrive around midday on Saturday and are broomed back out again before lunch on Sunday.

It was one of the few moments that felt like they made sense. Mikie and I were sitting in the parking lot just watching cars roll up. Just like we would have been doing at about this point any other summer at home.

"I bet your mother gets here before my mother," I said.

"Hnn," he said.

"I mean it, Mikie. What do you want to bet? I'll bet you anything."

"Cut it out, Elvin. I don't want to make bets on my mother."

"Fine, take another mother," I said. "I'll stack my mother up against any mother in the joint. Or any father. I bet she's the last one to show up. I bet I'm going to be sitting here with the crickets and the coyotes while everyone else is inside watching the talent show tonight and eating popcorn."

"She'll be here before Frankie's folks."

"No fair. *Jesus* will make an appearance before Frankie's folks do."

As I spoke, through the gate and up the drive came Mike's mother's little red Dodge Omni.

"See?" I said. "You owe me all your sick vouchers. Who's next? Who else wants to take on my mother? She's going to kick some big booty all over this camp."

Mike left me there ranting while he went to the car to greet his mother, Brenda. I could call her Brenda, because she always said I could. And that wasn't the only unmotherlike thing about her. She was smaller than us and red-headed and went on dates with men and did not mention it when one of our voices cracked even though everyone else in the world thought it was so damn funny. I was probably as anxious to see her when she stepped out of the car as Mikie was. As I always am.

She got out of the driver's side and hugged him, which I loved. I stood stupidly watching it for a few seconds.

Then I fell back down on the seat of my pants. Out of the passenger side popped—*my* mother.

I was cool. I got back up, walked super slowly to the Omni, and shook my mother's hand.

"This a new car, Brenda?" I asked while still shaking my mother's hand. Brenda waved me off, and Mom started laughing. She thinks every single thing I say is a laugh riot whether I intend it to be or not.

"Still at it, are we Elvin? I suppose you're chewing up everybody's slippers since I left you too."

Brenda came over and gave me a hug.

"Good," I said as she squeezed me to her. "*You'*ll take me home now, won't you?"

"You putting on weight?" she asked, holding me at arm's length.

"Yes, he is," Mikie chipped in unsolicited.

I pointed at myself as I spoke. "I'm in an athletic *pro gram*," I enunciated. "I'm bulking up."

"And *down*," Mike said.

Mom came up beside me and put an arm over my shoulders for moral support. I tried to be cool to her without scaring her off.

"So I have added a few pounds since I've been here. But I tell you, it's the training. Muscle weighs more than fat, you know."

"Ya, but a whole lot of fat still weighs more than a medium amount of muscle," Mike said.

"You look wonderful," my mother said, squeezing me.

"Strapping," Brenda said.

It worked. I felt wonderful and strapping, and gave Mikie a face that said so. Sometimes I think he gets a little jealous because I'm needier than him and the mothers mother me a little more out of instinct.

"Well, now that the size of my butt is out of the way," I said, "should we show you around?"

Mikie offered his arm, and Brenda took it. Mom looked at me expectantly.

"I knew you'd come crawling back," I said, hooking my arm for her like the little teapot short and stout.

"I always do, don't I?" she said, taking it.

The tour was somehow even duller than I'd figured it would be. There's the golf course, uh-huh uh-huh, there's the gym. It was goofy and bizarre on top of that, to be passing all the other guys giving the same stiff pointless tour to their parents, all of us pointing out the various activity areas on the day when no activities were being held. Yup, there's the baseball diamond, uh-huh uh-huh, there's the pool they don't let us swim in, uh-huh uh-huh.

The mothers were being polite about the whole thing, being dragged out three hours from home to be bored stupid. But after a while I couldn't take it. Even though it was against the rules, I found myself stumbling over into the truth.

"There's where the football coach made all the linemen run wind sprints after supper and I threw up baked beans into my nose. Couldn't breath for twenty-four hours."

"Oh, it never happened," my mother said, punching me on the shoulder.

"Oh yes it *did*," I said through gritted teeth as I punched her back. I thought I hit her hard. She laughed some more.

"And over there is where I woke up in the middle of the night, *in* that frog-infested stagnant pond, *in* my bed, which must have taken ten of them to move out there so carefully."

"Stop, stop it, Elvin," Mom protested. "You're killing me."

"I was only happy that there were those kindly eight million mosquitoes to roust me, or god knows what else that rabid, in-heat raccoon would have done to me next."

"Mikie," Brenda said, "did *any* of this actually happen to him?"

Mike shrugged. "I've totally lost track. Some of it seems to be confirmed by what I hear around camp, other stuff I don't know. I really doubt the one about the peanut butter and the shaved opossum."

"It *happened*," I snapped. Then I turned to the mothers. "But I don't want to talk about it."

We walked down to the track-and-field area, where there was a sort of reception for the parents, with games and a light barbecue snack.

The barbecue was embarrassing. They set out a huge metal bowl full of corn bread made out of dust, a couple of buckets of apples that when you bit into them turned out to be apple sauce cleverly wrapped up in apple skins, and a rack of spare ribs that were only spare because they were left on the floor after some pig's liposuction operation. You could have sailed a boat on the ocean of fat. Nobody ate any of it.

There was one popular item, however.

Right next to the two picnic tables covered in red and white checks were two big Rubbermaid trash barrels full of beer and ice. This, apparently, was for the fathers, because they lined up like they were going to communion as Brother Jackson, the official spirits dispenser, *ho-ho*ed them up. As each father—with his boy yanked to his side—shuffled up grinning and mumbled about the greatness of the school and the football team and the camp and the trees and god, Brother Jackson bowed a sort of benign grinning blessing and slapped a cold one into his hand.

It was all the gung-ho slottists and their likewise square-jawed daddies who did that. No normal families. No women. The point seemed to be to separate THEM from, well, sub-THEMs. A nod, a wink, a quick chugalug, and we had order.

And a party. The plan worked beautifully. Shortly after the fathers passed through the beer line once, then twice, there was action. Three-legged races. Touch football. Water-balloon tosses. They even ate the ribs.

Brother Jackson stood there taking it all in, smiling, smiling, nodding, waving, making out the little mental lineup card for the next four years.

"Why not?" I heard Brenda say.

"You think so?" my mother answered.

And off they went.

"Oh my god!" I said to Mikie. "Can't you do something? Stop them."

"Why?" he said, grinning as he watched Brother Jackson reluctantly hand over two beers to the ladies.

"What is she doing?" I said. "She doesn't drink beer. You don't drink beer," I said as she returned. "You go give that back right this minute."

"Hush, Elvin," Mom said.

I looked on, horrified, as my mother chipped her long perfect nails picking at the top of that filthy beer can.

"Here, let me get that for you," Mikie said, ever the frigging gentleman.

"Thank you, Mike," she said, and . . . I watched her little bit of an Adam's apple flick four times as she held the can up. *Four* times. The can was up there for, like ten minutes.

"Want me to run and get your toga out of the car, Ma?" I asked, arms folded.

"Oil your hinges, will you, Elvin?" Brenda said, and gave me a shove. She pushed me a few feet back.

I returned. "Oh, come on," Ma said, putting her arm around me and forcing me to sit at the picnic table with her.

"See, *they*'re drinking iced tea," I said, indicating the other mothers.

"Until Monday when their husbands go back to work."

"Well, at least they make the eff—"

"Elvin, have a piece of corn bread. You love corn bread."

"I'm not hungry. I had a big breakfast."

"That was hours and hours ago. And you're still not hungry? What did you eat?"

"I'm in training. I just have to watch it, that's all."

"Oh, I see," she said. And she did see. She didn't see it all, but she saw enough to know to leave it alone.

A football came spinning end over end our way, skidded across the table, and landed under Mom's bench. She sipped her beer, reached for the ball.

"All right. Right here, lady," guys from both teams hollered at her, clapping their hands.

"Throw it long," Brenda called.

"Give it to me—I'll walk it over," I said.

She wound up, big like a baseball pitcher, her left foot immodestly high in the air, and let it fly.

The ball went straight up in the air, landed on the picnic table, bounced off the corn bread without chipping a single piece, then rolled meekly to the ground. Mikie picked it up and sailed it back while all the real men laughed and joked and applauded.

"Who was that? Sign her up," one kid yelled.

Another kid, one of the chosen ones I recognized from my football days, called out an answer. "Couldn't you tell? That's Elvin's father," he yelled.

"Can we go now?" I asked very quietly but very firmly. "Can we, please?"

Mom nodded, and as we started walking, Mikie and Brenda joined us. "So where are we going?" Brenda asked.

"Someplace better than this," I said. "A special Sector where only the coolest guys are allowed. The library."

"We have a library?" Mikie laughed.

"Yes, but usually I'm the only one allowed in. I'll make an exception for parents' weekend, though."

"So," Mom said when we'd put a little distance between them and us, "do you still really hate it here that badly?"

"Sure do," I said.

"Well, you can come home if you want to. I'm glad you tried it, but if you don't want to stay the last week, you can come home with Brenda and me tomorrow."

I gave it time, as if I was thinking it over, even though I wasn't. I didn't want her to feel rejected. "No. Thanks anyway," I said evenly.

"I'm proud of you, Elvin. I really am," she said, and she took my hand.

"Ah, you're drunk," I said, squeezing.

I turned on only a couple of lights in the library. It was darker and more musty and beautiful than before. Mikie was awed at what was here that nobody even knew about. We didn't do much, except browse almost silently in four different directions for an hour. Maybe two hours.

I figured they all loved it as much as I did when the Nightmeal gong rang in the tower and I had to flash the lights on and off for ten minutes to collect everybody up again.

"This is the finest group we have ever had in all my years as headmaster," Brother Jackson boomed. The audience stomped their feet and whacked their glasses with silverware and *woof-woof*ed as if they truly believed Jackson did not say that to last year's group and wouldn't be saying it to next year's.

147

We were assembled at long tables in the dining hall, trying to eat our community meal and watch the stage at the same time. The ribs had returned. And the corn bread. The tablecloths too, that were supposed to get our all-American appetites pumped up. In an effort to keep us all from starving totally to death and leaving them with a big mess to clean up, they had also added hot dogs, hamburgers, and corn on the cob, all apparently boiled in the same gigantic vat. And finger bowls of their own secret barbecue sauce which, it was no secret, was ketchup mixed with vinegar and imitation maple syrup.

So the entertainment *had* to be good.

Part of what this was all about was to show the parents just what the administration could turn out in just a couple of weeks. Toward that end and "without further ado," as Brother Jackson said—

"Did we miss the earlier ado?" I didn't know where she was getting it, but Mom was developing a pretty smart mouth on her.

"I would like you all to see the future of Knights' powerhouse football," Jackson bellowed, clapping heartily right into his microphone so that it sounded like we were being shelled.

And out onto the stage marched the football team. In full, gleaming red-and-white home uniforms. There were twenty-two of them, representing a full offensive and defensive unit, and it was just for show, but you could bet that these same guys would wind up somewhere in that school football program in the near future.

Probably wearing the numbers they'd already chosen.

"Of course"—Jackson leaned into his microphone, all smirk and smart-ass—"this is just a show. Since this is not a real"—he dragged out the word, reeeeeeal, winking—"football camp, we don't *really* know that much about the ability of these particular boys. But come the fall, they'll have their chance just like everybody else."

The kids looked like a real football team. The Dallas Cowboys.

No, the Oakland Raiders.

"They frighten me," Mom whispered.

"Ya, well they don't scare me," I whispered even more softly.

As the not-really-the-football-team thundered offstage right (well of course—they wore their cleats for the show), the Arroyo brothers bounded up the left side. A pair of soccer-playing twins who had just moved with their physician parents from Spain, the Arroyos *had* to be a part of the show. They were a major prize. The Knights beat out several other local Catholic schools in a savage competition to win the white-blond scholar-athletes to beef up the soccer program. Never mind that the school's soccer program falls somewhere behind bocce ball in the hierarchy of team sports. Forget that they had to hustle to get enough kids to qualify as a team and thus provide the Arroyos with a forum for their skills. The Arroyos were a high-profile acquisition for a school that made the front page of the metro section after an investigation into the "complexion" of their scholarship programs.

So what if, as Mikie observed, "They must've had to *boil* those two to bleed all their color out? They're whiter than *you*, Elvin."

I happen to be fair skinned. To the point where you can see into me like the muscle chart in the doctor's office.

They were a catch, and they were going on that stage. It was a bonus that they could also keep a ball in the air for a half hour without letting it hit the floor.

Which they did. It was a boring half hour, but it gave us a chance to eat and was a big public relations score for the school.

Until he spoiled it.

The Arroyos were nearing the big finale, heading the ball back and forth and back and forth, faster now and faster, actually getting people to look up from their plates as the ball pinballed between them, when . . .

Zzziiiip. He came howling from backstage. Absolutely naked. Except for a skimpy little Zorro mask. He split into the middle of the boys, grabbed the ball.

"No hands," one of the boys called automatically. "Cannot use the hands."

He tossed the ball up, headed it a few times himself, keeping pretty fair balance, then ran out from under it, disappearing back the way he came.

The bouncing of the ball echoed through the quiet hall as everyone sat. Then a few guys started whistling. A few more started clapping. A few fathers joined in, until half the crowd was cheering, the other half muttering. He didn't have the vocal support of most guys' mothers, but they didn't look entirely upset either as they whispered amongst themselves.

"Was that Frankie?" my mother finally said, making me gulp.

"When did he get so hairy?" Brenda asked.

The answers were: Yes, it was Frankie; and last summer was when he got hairy. He was cruising through his O's apprenticeship now. Too bad his folks couldn't be there to see.

"I am sorry," Jackson said, and hustled the next act on. This was a stroke of genius, since they were so awful they certainly must have bored everyone into total amnesia. It was counsellors, athletes, mostly team captains. Each one came out to tell in drippy detail how awesome his team was, how awesome the school was, how awesome sports would be for the kids, how awesome it was to have spirit, and how awesome his own personal coach was. The only ones who didn't make you wish you had a gun with a scope on it were the football and hockey guys, who were drunk and in a rush to get back up to the campsite. We could hear, loud and clear, the sound of Obie throwing up as soon as he left the stage.

"You don't do that, do you, Elvin?"

"You know I don't drink, Ma."

"No, I mean the nudity thing that Frankie did."

"Ma," I said scoldingly. I turned red just from hearing her say it, never mind doing it.

"I know. It's just that, well, I understand that there are certain pressures sometimes, to do things in unfamiliar situations that you might not normally do. That's all. I just want you to be aware . . . that's all."

"I'm aware," I said.

"And to represent our fine wrestling program . . ." My ears pricked up at the sound. I hadn't heard anything about this.

". . . could Elvin Bishop come backstage please? Also, could . . ."

I was stunned breathless. I looked to my mother. I looked to Mikie. Nobody had an answer to this one. A proud little smile slipped across Mom's face, and there was no longer a choice. I had to go.

Backstage. "How come nobody told us about this?" I asked as I cautiously stepped into my suit.

"It was all thrown together last minute," the mean and quiet wrestling counsellor said. He was big and round muscled and wouldn't look me in the eye. We almost never saw him at the Sector, and when we did, he would only work with the real wrestlers, like Axe. "Wrestling makes a good show," he said. "It works onstage too. We can't exactly have a goddamn baseball game up there while your parents are eating."

"I guess we can't," I said.

Other wrestlers came in and dressed. Axe, Metzger, whoever got called over the P.A. Mostly the hard cores.

I started to worry. Could it be this bad? Were they so deranged in this place that bloodshed would actually be considered part of a nice dinner-theater show? I turned to watch from the side as two of the little guys put on a fine exhibition, grappling away in front of the crowd. Technically, they were beautiful. One leg wrapped around another, a clean takedown. A half nelson. An escape. They knew exactly what they were doing, and twined around each other like one animal. A boa constrictor.

The crowd applauded heartily when they were done, and again after the next two, also small guys. I applauded too. That was the way it was supposed to be done. That was what they were up there for.

What was I doing up here?

"And now a special treat . . ."

"This should be good," I thought, lost in the show now.

"The Masked Potato versus Little Death!"

Huh?

Then somebody, two somebodies, two big somebodies who stank like beer, grabbed me from behind. One wrapped me up in a bear hug, then the other jammed a sheer nylon stocking over my head.

The place erupted with laughs when they shoved me mightily out onto the stage, where I was met by my opponent, the dwarf. He ran full steam, jumped into the air, bounced off my chest.

I didn't know what was going on, but the audience sure was loving it. I tried, dazed, to look around for answers, but every time my eyes left him, the strong little bastard slammed me, so I had to fight, sort of.

I tried to grab him, to contain him, but he ran. I chased him around the periphery of the stage, but I couldn't get him—he ducked low to the ground and ran such tight circles that I just couldn't manage. Then he got around me and kicked me in the behind.

I thought the hall was going to cave in on us with the wild, on-its-feet cheering of the crowd. I looked to Brother Jackson for some sort of unspoken explanation. He pretended not to see me.

Then Little Death jumped up on my back, holding me around the neck.

"I swear I'm going to kill you," I said as his cheek pressed up against mine. I clutched desperately at his face.

"Cut the shit," he said through quick shallow breaths. "Just do the damn show."

"Why?" I asked, wheezing from his choke.

"I want to get along," he said.

I reached him, caught his hair. I gave it all the hate I had, which right then was more hate than anybody, when I pulled him down over my head and slammed him on the floor.

He was tough. He didn't even seem to mind what I did, or when I landed on top of him. He just wanted me to get it.

"I had to say yes," he went on as I tried lamely to force his shoulders to stay down. "Guy like me . . . guy like you. Best you can do. Be a sport. You get along."

More than ever I wanted him down. I wanted to slam him. But I couldn't do it.

Then I looked up, into the crowd. I was so lost, I didn't

even know what I felt about it. I needed to read my mother's face.

I was frightened by what I saw. She was frightened. She was scared and sad and looking to me like she might cry except that she was so totally confused. That was it, the problem was that she didn't know. She might cry in a second, if I let her know. Or she might laugh if I didn't.

When he gave me the tiniest shove, I flew off Little Death like I was slung from a catapult. My fans gobbled it up. I stood in classic ready position as he then came stalking me.

"Now you get it," he said quietly. "It's better this way. Come on, you've seen it a million times on TV—let's go for it."

He rushed me, punched me, not hard, in the solar plexus, and I doubled over. When I did, he grabbed me in a headlock. I straightened up, with him still clinging to me, and walked all around the stage.

"Where is he?" I demanded of the crowd, as if I didn't know he was hanging off my face. I turned all around, spinning us both in a circle until I got dizzy and we fell in a heap.

We got up and did some more of the tried-and-true big-fat-guy-chasing-little-dwarfy-guy shtick, him running between my legs, then when I bent over to look between them, him leapfrogging over my back. The kid was a great athlete.

By the time he finally pinned me a couple of long minutes later—me lying flat on my back with my arms and legs jerking like a heart patient getting electrical jolts—we had them all roaring with laughter.

I got up and we shook hands to the background music of applause, but we could not look at each other. As we made our way off the stage, Brother Jackson held out his happy hand for me to shake. I walked right by him.

My mother was still awestruck after I'd changed into my regular clothes and returned to the table.

"I have never seen that side of you, Elvin. You've become a real cutup. What have they done to you here?"

I didn't even touch it. If she was happy, I was happy. I smiled nice. Mike smiled nice too. He knew.

The kids' parents with dough stayed at the hotel or one of the bed and breakfasts in town. The rest stayed in the dorms at the seminary. Mom and Brenda shared a room there.

We walked to the dorm to pick them up in the morning and carry their bags back to the car.

"Very gallant of you two," Brenda said, "dropping the girls off at the dorm at the end of the evening, *going home*, then coming back to pick them up in the morning. Remember that when you're in college."

"College?" I put my hand over my heart. "Could we slow down please? It was just a few weeks ago we were perfectly content in that school it had taken us eight years to get used to . . . then this . . . then *that* school in September . . . now the college thing. This is just too much, it's just to much."

My mother and Brenda laughed and laughed, as if I

was putting on yet *another* show for them. I wasn't.

They were leaving is what it was.

When we reached the car, I took Brenda's bag from Mikie and brought it along with Mom's around to the back. I popped open the Omni's hatch, threw in one bag, threw in the other, then climbed in after them. I wedged myself in between the luggage and the spare-tire compartment, flattened myself out, and pulled the hatch shut on myself.

The three of them came back at once. They stood there staring in at me, smiling broadly like I was something in a pet-store window. From my end, breathing was already a little hard.

Mikie looked back up over his shoulder, cupping a hand against the brilliant sun. It was already beating in on me through the glass.

"Remember what we used to do to frogs with a magnifying glass?" he asked. "You'll never make it home."

Brenda popped the hatch open. It made that hydraulic *pffffft* sound. Although that may have been me. "You are too funny, Elvin," she said.

"Too," Mom echoed, offering me a hand to get out. It was a struggle, much harder than getting in was, but together we extricated me. Mikie and his mom walked around to the driver's side, I and mine to the passenger's.

"Why don't you go and get your bag, Elvin," she said. "We can wait."

I looked over the top of the car at Mikie and Brenda hugging.

"Thank you very much for coming, Mrs. Bishop," I said. "I trust you enjoyed your stay here at the Rancho Diablo retreat. All our guests have a fine time, whether they like it or not, and we do hope you will return." I smiled good and cheesy and shook her hand.

"See you next week," she said, as bravely as I did. Then, as I was shutting her door, she whispered, "*Very* proud. I love you."

"There ya go now," I said, slamming the door hard. "On your way. Drive careful. And watch that drinking now."

We stood and watched them go. They all thought it was a joke, when the truth was it took everything I had to pull myself out of the back of the car.

But she was proud of me.

When the red Dodge Omni had finally disappeared, Mikie slapped me on the back. "Want to go get something to eat?" he asked cautiously.

I shook my head.

"You want to just hang out?"

I nodded.

"You want me to leave you alone?"

I shook my head.

"Library might be cool."

I nodded, and we started walking.

We could do that, sometimes for hours, times when things weren't so good for me. Me not saying a word the whole time and Mikie not making me. It took us years to get that just right, and now it sure made things a lot easier.

Chapter 9

Good-bye, Potato.

Ma,

I suppose this letter will beat you home by a couple of days since I imagine you and Brenda have been *Thelma and Louise*ing it across the countryside. But isn't it nice to know that *I* at least am still thinking about *you*?

I regret that this cannot be a long letter, but I must get to work. Your visit really threw off my training (so it's true, women weaken an athlete's legs), and I have a stiff week ahead. Coach has been matching me with smaller and smaller wrestlers until we locate somebody I can actually defeat, and if I continue at my current pace, I'm scheduled for an exhibition match on Friday against the spring lamb we're eating on Saturday.

Early betting's running about eight to five for the lamb. But I've seen him, and he doesn't look that tough.

Wish me luck.

And while you're at it, wish me skill and strength and bravery.

Elvin

Monday morning, I was paired with—well why not?—the dwarf. This time for real. I boned up on Rummy. I hung on to everything Eugene tried to remind me of. None of it rooted.

This was not the same dwarf who had played the game for the circus crowd on Saturday night. This was a dwarf who knew how to wrestle. He was strong and elusive. He was nasty. And he had something to prove—to me.

He threw himself at me, bounced off, came at me again. He grabbed my leg and nearly upended me, but I got my foot down, stomping his foot. He grabbed my leg again—the way a pit bull lunges and snaps and clamps and tears at the same piece of leg over and over—got it up, backed me up, then reversed direction. Now I was following him, hopping, trying not to fall. With a surge, he reversed me again, tipping me now, dumping me.

When I was down, he jumped on me. He grabbed my arm, pulled it up over my head. Then he was kneeling over me, pulling the arm up and digging his knee into my side.

"Punishing hold," Coach yelled, but the kid wouldn't break it. "Punishing hold!" Coach yelled louder, and the kid pulled harder on my arm. Tears came to my eyes, and some nerve thing happened so that I couldn't wiggle my fingers. The arm now went right past my head, to where I couldn't even see the elbow in my peripheral vision.

"Ow," I said. "Hey," a little more loudly, as if he would now notice my pain and let up. As if we were somehow on the same side of something. He made small straining grunt sounds as he tried to push my arm up farther, to snap it off.

Somehow I rolled. I got away, my deadened arm flopping after me. He jumped on me again when I was halfway up.

"Takedown," Coach yelled. "Come on, Elvin, break out of it."

It was beyond a takedown. I was on all fours, two palms pushing off the floor, one knee down, and one foot down, when he caught me, hooked an arm up under my crotch, and slammed me down, just like a rodeo calf roping.

"Come on, Elvin," Eugene yelled.

"Come on, Elvin," the dwarf snarled.

But I couldn't. Everyone in camp could have jammed the hall and started cheering for me. I could have reread Rummy Macias a hundred and fifty times. Rummy himself could show up in my corner and shout instructions, and it would make no difference. I was on the bottom, and I was staying on the bottom.

The two minutes were up, and the whistle blew ending round one. It was a formality. To start round two, I won the coin toss and took the top. The dwarf got down like a dog, I crouched over him, grabbing his arm and waist, and the whistle blew again.

Whomp. I was down quicker, harder than before. The dwarf was on top of me. But my shoulder was up. He slammed it down, snarling at me. I got the other one up. He slammed that one.

"Predicament," Coach called, which made the dwarf angrier and more determined. He kept slamming, and I kept slithering, but I would not have this mean, tiny, angry person pinning me to the floor. He could have the rest, but he couldn't have that.

After another tedious minute of this, Coach Wolfe called it off. As the dwarf got up off me, he pushed my face away hard.

"You're the joke," he spat. "I'm not the joke. You're the joke. I'm not the joke. You're the joke."

"Fine. So how come you're not laughing?" I said, slapping my arm back to life as he stalked away.

"Elvin?" Coach said after I'd had a few minutes' rest. "Elvin, you got enough in you to go another round or two?"

I felt myself nodding. I was getting this feeling of time running out on me as my body broke down. I wanted this. I wanted to find out more about me before I had to ride out the rest of camp on a voucher.

My next opponent was soft. He was light. He was scared. He was a little fat kid, as opposed to a big fat kid, definitely heavier than the bantamweight class they had him in, but it would have been cruel to put him any higher. I liked him immediately.

We locked. My hand was clapped around the back of his neck, his around mine. We leaned on each other's shoulders and pushed back and forth.

"You want to pin me?" he whispered.

"Huh?"

"My name's Lennox, and I'm out of here. I'm quitting. This is it for me. So I don't care. You want to pin me or you want me to pin you?"

I was mortified. "I want to *fight*, that's what I want." I backed him up across the ring.

He sighed a bored, disgusted sigh. "Spare me, all right? The only question is which one of us wants to not lose less than the other one." He pushed me back the other way.

I almost fell down just trying to follow the sentence, then I recognized what he was saying. He was describing the thing I had developed in my week-plus as a wrestler: back-ass desire.

"I want to win," I said, "but if you take a dive, I will not fall on top of you."

It had become a mighty struggle of antiwill. I wouldn't let him pin me. I wouldn't let him pin himself. I was in all likelihood incapable of pinning him. It would be a long three rounds.

Smack. He slapped me in the face.

"That'll cost you a poi—" Coach half yelled when I went off.

I pushed, and slapped, and cuffed, and choked, and butted Lennox across the ring, where he fell in a heap. Where I dropped on top of him, bounced, and flailed on top of him.

After a few pointless seconds, Lennox had to instruct me.

"Here, grab this leg. Grab this arm. Apply weight at this point. There you go. Jesus, Elvin, good job. No way I can get out of this."

"Try," I yelled in his face. "Try to break it, or I'll squish the shit out of you. I mean it."

He did. He pushed, and he pushed, and he pushed until his face turned the color of eggplant. He was there for good.

The whistle blew. "Pin!" Coach yelled, and sounded dumbfounded to do so. Eugene rushed over to congratulate me, and Lennox shook my hand. We were two oddly happy fat guys. He was happy to be done with wrestling, I was happy to have done something with it. A tiny something, but something.

As we sat eating Nightmeal, we were three sagging boys. We didn't really say much, other than "Pass the salt" and "You going to finish that?" July was never like this for us before. It was always September that was exhausting.

I sat as still as possible, trying to will away the shoulder pain that still made my pinky finger tingle, the headache, the new clicking in my ankles.

Mikie said it first. "Everyone knew it was you, Frankie, with all that hair all over your body."

"I don't think everyone knew," Frank said.

"My mother recognized you," I said.

"Well that's because your mother's seen me—"

"Don't you *dare*," I said, pointing a crooked index finger at him. He laughed.

"Couldn't you quit now, Frankie? I mean, haven't you been embarrassed enough? I think you've proved to them whatever it is you need to prove."

"I'm almost there," Frank said quietly.

"So what if you just said no more? You could hang out with us for the last week; we'd stick together day and night so they couldn't do anything to you." Mikie jerked his thumb over his shoulder at me. "As you know, the big El is getting pretty tough."

I attempted to raise both fists in the air as a sign of my erupting macho. But I couldn't get my arms up over my head.

"Thanks anyhow," Frank said with a little smile. "But I don't think they'll make me do anything else embarrassing. I think I'm in pretty good shape from here on in. Besides, you know, it's all in good fun."

Mikie shook his head at that, but for once didn't speak his superior mind. "Good luck then, Frank." He reached across the table and shook Frank's hand.

With all my strength I managed to reach out and flop my hand on top of their linked hands. A sort of Three Musketeers gesture.

As soon as we saw how it looked, we all felt the same.

"Jesus, this is stupid," Frankie said, pretty well capturing the moment. "Can we talk about something else anyway?"

Brother Jackson beat us to it.

"Every year," he said, with feedback screeching over the microphone, "we hope we don't have to do this. And every year, we do have to do it." He spoke grimly, as if what he had to do was announce the loss of a loved one, or direct us to the gas chambers. He shook his head slowly and dramatically. "Perhaps some of you did not take me very seriously when I talked to you of taking the measure of the man during this retreat. Perhaps you did not see, as we do, the *importance* of finding one's slot, finding one's way, in the big system. Well, it's been two weeks now, and I must say we have seen the measure of many of you, and you measure up impressively. We have seen the measure of others, and . . . well we don't know.

"Let me say it again, gentlemen: If we don't have a slot for you, what are we going to do with you?

"Do not try to answer, as that was a rhetorical question. But let me get to the thing I do not like to do. The reports are coming in that we have an overabundance of young men who are flatly washing out of the healthy and productive and character-building conventional slots we have set up for you. So we are forced to open up what we call the 'Alternative Slots.' Now, this does not mean that you people are any lesser than those men who will remain

166

in the football and baseball slots. It just means you're . . . a different sort."

I could feel it coming. I was already shaking my head no when Coach Wolfe stepped up from behind and put a hand on my shoulder. "Elvin. Can I talk to you a minute?"

He walked me out onto the verandah of the dining hall. I followed solemnly. I knew that when I reentered that hall, I would be going back as a mere diner like the rest of them, and never again as a Grappling Knight.

". . . I really do, Elvin, I wish I had more guys with your heart. I have never had a kid who hit the deck so damn easy, and then was so damn hard to pin. You should be proud of that. But the body just ain't willin'. I'm convinced that if I don't move you, you're going to get hurt somethin' awful."

Well what do you know, Coach; I just did get hurt somethin' awful. Who'd have guessed it?

I didn't share it with him, though. I stared past him, over his head, almost straight up over his head, at the Massachusetts Indian flapping away from the flagpole.

"Elvin?"

"That all, Coach?"

"Uh, ya, that's it. So . . . you okay with that?"

"I'm okay with that." And if I wasn't, I wouldn't tell you.

"All right. It's just that . . . I thought I might have seen something . . . that maybe you wouldn't be okay with it."

"Well," I said, looking down from the flag and into

his face now, "you were wrong, Coach. I never wanted to be in any wrestling slot. The whole thing was kind of a big fat joke anyhow, right? Why should I miss it? Get me out of here. Can I go back to dinner now?"

He shrugged.

On my way back in, I ran into Jackson coming out through the door. He put a hand on my chest.

"We have good sports here," he said coldly, addressing the sky as much as me. "You've got to learn to be a sport. Sportsmanlike. It's an important trait in the developing young man. Remember when you refused my hand? Up on the stage . . . in front of so many people?" He shook his head slowly, many times. "Very unsporting." He took his hand off me and walked on past.

I walked numbly into the dining hall, and before returning to the table, I went up and pulled another whole dinner to add to the one I already had.

"Think maybe I'll take a day off tomorrow," I said as I started power-chowing two meals.

Mikie turned to look at me. My hands were dancing over both trays the way a monkey handles peanuts.

"You got cut."

"Mmmm," I grunted, nodding.

"Sorry," he said.

"Why? I don't care. Why should I care? It's stupid. Already forgot about it. Do I look like I care? Do you *think* I should care? If wrestling was so hot, why weren't *you* down there sweating all over the mats and reading that moronic book for a week?"

"Okay," he said, and turned back to face Frank.

"The only thing that pisses me off," I snapped, grabbing Mikie by the arm, "is that I fell for it. Like a jerk. I can't believe I fell into that bullshit slotting trap. Slots! Shithead," I said, and smacked myself in the forehead.

"El," Frank said, grabbing my hand before I hurt myself somethin' awful just like Coach Wolfe predicted. "You come with me tomorrow. I'll get you in Golf Sector."

"Are you joking?" Mikie laughed.

"I have to go where they send me," I said. "And I'm sure they won't be sending me to the country club. Besides, it doesn't matter. There is no difference. Every slot is exactly the same as every other slot. That's what I learned."

He shook his head smartly. "Oh no they're not. The rest of them might all be the same, but not *mine*."

"Okay, fine, not yours," I said, taking a perfect round white potato off of Mikie's plate and popping it whole into my mouth without even asking. "But still, it's the last place they're going to send me."

"Consider yourself sent," Frank said. "*I'm* reassigning you."

"You have that kind of power?" Mikie asked, suspicious.

"Now you're catching on," Frank said. "It's not all for nothing, getting in with the right group."

"Don't do it, El," Mikie said. "They're just going to turn you into a counsellor toady, like . . . ." He jerked a silent thumb in Frank's direction.

Frank wasn't the easiest guy to offend; you really had to work at it. But this bothered him, that Mikie didn't seem to grasp just what status Frank had attained. It was a very important point with him.

"You *refuse* to give me any credit at all," Frank steamed. "You want to know what it's about? I'll tell you. I'm *chosen*, all right? You see who these guys are, the big ones like Obie? You might not like them, but they're the top of the hill around here. And now, when they move on, guess who the next top of the hill is? That's right, your old buddy Frank."

Frankie paused in his speech, waiting for some new appreciation from Mike. It was too slow coming.

"Come on, Mikie. I'm being groomed, they tell me. Of all these guys here, I'm picked to carry on the tradition. There is a big tradition at this school, and tradition means everything. This is how it happened with Obie and those guys before, and with the guys who came along before that. This *means* something. I'm going to be a real somebody in this picture. And you guys are going to be there with me if you want. It's going to be the coolest time . . ."

"Maybe he knows what he's talking about, Mike," I said, even though I doubted it. But the whole scene was getting to me. "Maybe Franko's going to turn out to be a genius, and you're going to just be one more slot monkey."

Frankie got up and went to meet his buddies, like he did every night now. But he looked a little less beat than he had the last few nights. "Tomorrow," he said, pointing at me and winking.

"Maybe," I said. "I'll let you know in the morning."

Mike stared at me.

"What?" I said. "It might be fun. You know, Mike, maybe Frank's right. You don't have to be so stiff all the time."

He didn't respond at all. So I finished my dinners. Then I finished his. "I have to go," I said, taking all three trays to the dumper. "I have to go finish something."

I left him there and went back to the Cluster. When I got there, it was empty except for Thor, who was waiting on my bed.

"Elvin, remember what Brother Jackson said about 'If you don't have a slot, then what are we going to do with you?' Well he's the kind of guy who picks his words carefully, y'know? It wasn't an idle question—it was more like a warning."

"Why are you here, Thor?" I asked.

"I'm here because I like you, and I want to help you get along."

"And because you've been spoken to? About me?"

"Don't be paranoid. We get spoken to about everybody, in one way or another. Evaluations are just a part of the program. The thing is, you want to get along, Elvin. You don't have to love everything about the school—I don't love it all myself. But I learned. I learned how to play. You don't have to love the slotting thing, but trust me, you don't want to be alone either. When Jackson says, 'You'll never get anywhere in this world without your slot,' what he means is 'You'll never get anywhere in *this world*.'" As he said it, Thor pointed with both index fingers at the floor under us—meaning where we're at now.

I walked past him, picked up my wrestling book, and tucked it under my arm.

"Thanks," I said, I wasn't sure for what. I'd figure it out later, but for now it felt like he was doing something nice for me, and I should appreciate it.

"Make yourself some friends. Some other guys like yourself," Thor said, laughing a friendly laugh at the ridiculousness of that last part. "I've seen it every way here. Seen some guys work it right, seen other guys do not such a good job of it. You don't want to just not fit when you get to this school, Elvin. Believe me, you don't want that."

"Okay, Thor," I said as I walked out the door. I said it like a wiseguy because that was the way to handle it. But I took him seriously all the same. "I'm going right now. I'm gonna hit the trail and round me up some friends." I started calling out to the surrounding hills, "Yo! Yoooo-hooooo. Friends? Where are you, friends? Come on now, you can't hide from me forever."

When I got to the library, I didn't flip on the lights once I was inside. I just found my way to the stack where I knew the Rummy book belonged. I thought I was just going to slip it back into place. But I didn't. First I ripped off the front cover. Then the back. Then I tore out the intro page with the stupid "Every boy yearns for a good tussle" sermon. Then I ripped the book in half at the spine, threw the halves on the floor, picked them up again, tore out one page, two, three, four, five, six. Threw them up in the air.

I couldn't let it go.

I tore out more pages. Crumpled them. Picked them back up, picked up the covers. Cracked the covers over my knee. Slapped it all together in one big trash sandwich, and jammed it back in the stack.

I figured it wouldn't be missed. You'd have to be a loser to come looking for that book anyway.

Then I went quietly to the librarian's raised desk in the middle of the main room. I sat down, clicked on the single brass desk lamp, found a pen and paper, and wrote.

Mom,

So what about this home schooling thing? Ever hear of it? What do you know about it? Why wasn't I informed before? Am I too old? Is it too late for me? Please investigate.

But that's the future. As for right now, I'm nowhere. I closed out my wrestling career—you saw me at my zenith, I must say—by cascading down the weight classes in search of a lighter, weaker opponent. By the merciful end I was losing to guys who weighed less than my bathing suit does when it's wet. It was really stupid, the whole wrestling thing, and you know what? I don't even miss it. I don't feel a thing. I am embarrassed, but not because they ran me *out* of wrestling, but because I was *in*. I was so stupid for a week. I told you this camp was no good for me. I was a lot of things before I came here. I was a lot of grotesque things. But I was never stupid. You must admit that, Ma, that I was never stupid. So see? See what happened to me here?

But I'm better now. To answer your question, no, I'm not upset and I'm not bothered, and I don't miss it.

And I don't miss home. I don't miss watching TV movies with you, and eating supper off my lap. And I don't miss walking six blocks to the convenience store together every night after supper because we pretended to forget some small and stupid thing when we did the big weekly shopping. I don't miss that long slow walk to Henry's, past the American Legion baseball game under the lights to get a box of brown sugar or Kleenex or Comet and then get a blue slush at Larry's next door for the walk back home. I mean, what kind of way is that to spend a hot July night anyway?

And I don't miss my friends, who are here, but it isn't the same as being home in beautiful boring July with them, doing more nothing than ever, which is when we are best together. It isn't the same with them, because . . . I'm not sure why. But something is happening here and it is very frightening to me the way taping the windows before a hurricane is frightening to me, whether we ever get hit with the storm or not.

But I don't miss it.

And I don't miss you at all, Ma. I know I said that two paragraphs ago but sometimes, like during all the nights here when the black and quiet come in under the door for nobody but me, I feel like I don't say that as much as I should say it.

But I am not lonely as I free-fall down through the slots here, to a bottom that goes I don't know where because I am afraid to look down.

Got a net handy, Ma?

I am not lonely because I have these questions to keep me company. They stay with me the whole time, to make sure I'm never alone. Is there a slot for me? What do I do? Where do I go? Is there a place for me? Will anyone be there when I get there?

So you see I'm not lonely. I'm not lonely, and I don't miss anyone. Did it work, then? Am I who we wanted me to be when we sent me here? Am I flying, like the baby bird rolled out of the nest? Or am I free-falling? Is there a difference?

Oh, wait a minute, I just remembered. I'm a golfer. Never mind.

Elvin "Links" Bishop

Chapter 10

Golf and god.

I woke up the next morning and went bleary-eyed through my routine. Moaned and groaned. Stretched until something like non-Gumby human motion was possible. Lumbered out to do my run.

I slowed down. The naked eye probably could not tell, but I slowed down. Then I stopped, which was obvious. I didn't have to run. I was no longer a football player or a baseball player or a wrestler. I was, once again, a mere sloth. In fact I was beneath sloth—I was a golfer. I went back inside and slept another hour in my running clothes.

"Coming?" Frank asked, kicking my bed as he rubbed at his eyes with the heels of his hands. His voice was hoarse, his hair standing way up and all over like cotton candy.

"Ya, I'm coming," I said. "It's not like I'm here sorting through invitations, wondering which party to go to."

I sat up slowly and looked all around at the empty bunks and the last of the guys heading off to their Sectors. I'd outslept everybody, even Frankie. Breakfast was over already. "Will there be snacks?" I asked.

"I'll wait for you outside," he grogged. "I have to get outside. They'll have stuff; just don't talk about food to me now."

"Oh, what to wear, what to wear," I said into my sliver of a locker as Frank coughed and hacked and possibly up chucked in the background.

I laughed. First a little, then a lot. Frank heaved louder and I laughed harder. Not at him. I wasn't happy that he was hurting. It was just that, with that soundtrack playing for me as I clothes shopped, I realized how ridiculous this all was. Golf. Golfing with Obie. *Dressing* for golfing with Obie.

Frankie had been quiet for a while, until I came out the door. Bent over a rock, he looked at me, then started heaving all over again.

"What?" I asked, looking over my own ensemble. "Too much?"

I had on some of my "good" clothes that I had packed in case—I don't know, in case there was a dance or something, I guess. Pale yellow, wide-band polyester fat-man Sansabelt semi-dressy shorts that came down to just above the knee. White sandals, tan socks. And a screaming orange lifeguard T-shirt that I could not resist borrowing off of Thor's bed even though it was too tight and fit my belly like shrink-wrap. And his evergreen Green Bay Packers football hat that was really a baseball hat.

"You cannot come," Frank grunted through heaves. "This is the thanks I get for trying to hel— *Uuuuuuggghhgh. Bluaaaaaaaahhhhhggggghhhh.*"

"It's the orange and the tan together, then, huh? Is that the problem?"

"El," he said, wiping his mouth on the hem of his T-shirt, "if you don't go get that costume off, I'm going to throw up all over it."

I shook my head and folded my arms. "Nope. Sorry. I'm a golfer and this is what golfers look like. You invited me, so let's get moving."

He didn't make a sound, hardly even breathed. He just sat there in a heap on the ground staring at me, then began rubbing his eyes again. He was helpless to do anything about me.

"Help me up," he begged, sticking out his hand. When he was on his feet, he looked me over once more. "Fine. But you're on your own. Whatever they do to you, you asked for it."

"Can't be any worse than what they did to you," I said, walking ahead of him.

"*I* just had a lot of fun, that's all."

"Well then, I just hope whatever they do to me, it isn't any fun."

"Look," somebody yelled as soon as we made our

178

appearance over the hill. "Franko brought his own caddy. It's a chimp."

"Jesus," Obie said, smacking me on the chest. "You look like somethin' I puked up this mornin'."

They all *YUK-YUK-YUK* laughed.

"Oh no," I interrupted, "not if it was the same stuff Frankie puked up this morning. See, I'm yellow and orange, and Frank's puke was mostly brown and red."

They all thought that was even funnier than my outfit. Except Frankie, who turned on me. "Don't do it to me, Elvin." He grabbed me by the shirt and yanked me close to him, put his eyeballs almost up against my eyeballs, so his rancid breath mingled with my breath. "Not this morning," he said. "And not in front of these people. It'll be too much." He let go of my shirt when I shut completely up and lost the wiseguy part of my smile.

"Yo, Franko," Obie said, clapping him on the back. "Bet you could use one of these, after last night." He pulled a dripping cold yellow can of beer out of his golf bag. It was not yet nine-thirty A.M.

Obie held it right under Frankie's nose. I could see his eyes water. Which made my eyes water. His lips tightened. He produced instant sweat, on his lip, his brow, down along his sideburn areas. His skin turned the canary color of my shorts as Obie leered, continued to hold the beer there, and breathed his own probably wonderful breath in Frankie's face. He was holding on like a tiger, but Frankie wasn't going to make it through this, not another ten seconds.

"Give me that," I said, snatching the beer right out of Obie's hand. At first he looked like he was going to clock me, even took a step toward me as his buddies *oooohhh*ed at him to do it. But quick as I could, I ripped the top of the beer open, tipped it up, and started chugging.

"Whoa-whoa-whoa-whoa," they started chanting, for me. Just like in frat-party movies. I watched Obie out of the corner of my eye, to make sure this was working. It was. He was watching me as if I were coming up on the rail at the Kentucky Derby with all his money on my nose.

Glug-glug-glug . . . slam. I did it. Spiked the can in the dirt, and let rip with a burp that could have brought black bears down out of the hills to mate with me.

They loved me. Frank loved me best, though.

"Glad you came," he whispered, touching me lightly on the back. He looked better already. He was renewed.

"Get two more of those bad boys over here, will you?" he roared. "Jeez, we're thirsty guys, you know. Right, El? What, do they think they're playing with *kids* here?"

The beers arrived before I even had a chance to gag. With them came a slap on the back and a bag of golf clubs to schlep. Blindly I toddled after the pack, shaky and afraid.

"Now you're going the right way, El," Frank said.

"Am I?" I asked, looking all over the place desperately, without any idea what the right way was.

"Drink up, boys," Obie commanded from the front of the pack. "And get those clubs up here, goddammit."

"Drink up," Frank said, clapping his can against mine.

"Jesus, Frank," I said. "What time is it?"

"What time do you want it to be?" he asked, talking and laughing and drinking all at once so that the beer ran out of both corners of his mouth.

They wouldn't let me golf until I finished that beer. So I remained a caddy through the first and second and third holes. Then on the fourth tee I finished the beer and didn't *want* to golf anymore. I just wanted to sit down on the grass.

"Come on, Elvin," Frankie said, tugging me up by the shirt. "You can't sit there—you have to carry the bags."

By now we were both lugging around two whole sets of clubs belonging to the O's.

"No way," I said. "I'm sitting."

"You can't sit."

"Fine," I said, and lay down.

Frank rushed away from me, so as not to be tainted by the connection. I got up on my elbows and watched as he put the bags down and teed up. *Whack.*

I couldn't believe it. He was great. It sounded like the snap of a thick healthy tree branch breaking when he hit that ball. It sailed straight and long, thirty yards past the next-best drive. Golf. It was about the only thing Frank and his dad did together all the time.

"Nice shot, Franko," Obie said, punching Frank on the shoulder. "Now get those bags, will ya?"

The O's all loped along toward the fifth hole, unburdened by their own clubs. Unburdened by anything else, either.

"Come on, Elvin, get it going," Frankie said.

"This sucks worse than Football Sector."

"It does not," he said. "And it'll get a lot more fun later on, trust me. But for now, do your job. Privilege has to be earned, you know."

"No it doesn't, stupid. That's why they call it a privilege, because you don't do shit to get it. You just, you know, get it."

Frank was getting frustrated with me. "El, if they reach the next tee without their clubs . . . Come on. Please?" he asked anxiously as the O's left us behind.

"No. I quit." I fell back again. The dew on the grass felt awfully good on the back of my neck.

"You can't quit."

"Ha." It was my most supremely confident laugh. It was my *only* confident laugh. "Oh yes I can. There are many many things I cannot do. But quit? Quit I can, with the best of them. I quit football in the middle of the day, when everybody said it couldn't be done. I quit baseball so fast it made their helmets spin. Hell, I quit wrestling when I wasn't even *trying* to quit. It's frightening, the quitting powers I possess. Why, if they only had a Quitting Sector here, I'd be home free. I'd be the captain. I'd be the coach—"

"Well then do it for me. If you quit now, they'll probably make me carry all four bags."

I sat up to look at him, preparing something wiseguy to say to him. But when I saw his big stupid wet eyes, he looked soft and weak. That wasn't right. It wasn't Frank at all. He wasn't that way, ever, soft and weak. He wasn't that way, and he wasn't supposed to be.

"You quit too, then."

"Nope," he said, and gave up, started hoisting all four bags on his shoulders. He looked like a little tiny boy under them.

"All right, all right," I said, and took my share. We double-timed it to the fifth hole. "But why not?" I finally asked, just before we got there. "You don't need this."

"Yes I do," he said softly. "I'm almost there. I'm almost made."

No matter how many times he said it, no matter how hard he tried, Frankie couldn't quite make me see the magic of his arrangement. But what was clear to me was that he did see it. So I went along.

"Here you go, boys," Okie said, shoving two more beers in our hands.

The thought made me woozy. "Thank you anyway," I said, handing it back. "Got any Gatorade?"

"Don't be a wuss," Okie said, snarling and smiling at the same time.

"Just take it, Elvin," Frank whispered.

Okie monitored us, to make sure we didn't waste any of his expensive, imported New Jersey beer. The rest of them were watching us too. So I sipped.

Frankie didn't sip. He gulped. "What's the occasion?" he asked. "You guys don't usually have brew in the daytime."

They didn't usually, and they didn't now, either. They

were spectators, I realized. Frank and I were the show.

"Nothin' special," Obie called. "Headin' into the last week, we just thought it was time you advanced to the next level."

"Thanks," Frank said with a puzzled look. Then they all looked at me.

I had two full beers and a sip in my belly already. That was about one and a half more than I'd ever had in there at one time before. I was sweating. I was sleepy. My stomach was a little fluttery and dangerously empty of food. But it was up there in my head too. And I decided that two beers was not the worst feeling I ever had.

I drank down the third beer.

Three beers was the worst feeling I ever had.

We were on the road, halfway to the sixth tee, when I began unraveling. First I dropped one of the two golf bags. The strap slowly slid down my shoulder, down my arm, onto the ground. I was aware of it, felt it happening, but couldn't seem to react to it. And when it finally dropped, I left it. I kept walking, looked down at it once, kept walking, and never even considered stooping to pick it up.

Ten yards along, Frankie said, "Hey. Hey, Elvin. Go get that."

I turned to look at him and shook my head no. Then I let the second bag fall.

"Cut that out," he said in that now-familiar desperate whisper. Too late. We were noticed.

"What the hell's goin' on?" Odie hollered. "Get my damn clubs."

"Go," Frank said.

I did not reply, so Frank hooked his bags over my shoulders and went to claim mine. That satisfied the O's, so they resumed walking. As soon as they'd turned away, and before Frank reached the fallen clubs, I vomited. Loudly.

No, no one rushed to my aid. No one brought me a towel, or a drink of water. They booed. The O's simply all stood in a line as if the national anthem were playing, and they booed me while I puked.

"Clear him out of here, Frankie," Obie commanded. "And he was never here, Frank. Make sure of it. It didn't happen to him here."

Frank stood over me patiently, shielding me from the O's by standing between us. He waited until I was good and empty, then helped me to my feet, putting my arm over his shoulder. He didn't say anything until we were off the golf course, across the parking lot, and standing near the entrance to the administration building that housed the nurse's station. He removed his hand from around my waist, checked me out to see that I was steady on my own, then started walking backward away from me.

"I'm sorry, Elvin," he said, walking away slowly.

And as he said it, I wanted to cry. I felt even sorrier for him, watching him crawl back for more.

There are some things a guy just shouldn't have to see.

So this is how they get you. They got me good.

"No, Thor, this couldn't be right."

"They don't make mistakes when they hand down assignments. And even when they do make mistakes, they don't. If you know what I mean. So there you go, Friar."

Religion Sector. A.k.a. The Calling. This was what happened when they couldn't mold you into one of the preferred manly slots. And try as they might, they found me unmoldable. I retained my shape, such as it was.

"Okay, Thor, let's work on this one, huh? I've got no calling. None. God has never called to me personally, and if he did, frankly, I wouldn't answer. So this is a big fat mistake."

"Well, Elvin, this Sector is for more than just the guys who might want to go into the priesthood or brotherhood. There's also the opposite."

"Meaning?"

"What did you do yesterday, Elvin?"

"Damn!"

"See, you need help."

"Damn, damn, damn. How does everyone know everything around here?"

"You don't want to know that."

"Fine. Well anyway, I don't care anymore. About anything. So I don't want to go to any crappy Religion Sector, so I won't go. I'll swear all day if I have to, so they won't want me. Shit. Shit, goddammit."

Thor held his washboard abdomen laughing at me. "I am going to hate to see you leave, man. But seriously, this is a kind of plea-bargain thing. You go to Religious

Studies as a sort of alternative substance-abuse program, or they tell your mother what happened."

That shut me right up.

"Well what about *him*?" I said, pointing to Frankie, who was still detoxing in bed. I was so irritated, I didn't care what a rat I was being.

"*He* didn't turn himself in."

"Grrrr," I said.

"Yes, Elvin, grrr."

"Assholes."

"Well, yes."

"Damn them to hell."

"*Now* you're getting in the spirit."

"Where do I go?" I sighed.

"Gymnasium basement," he said.

"Of course." I slunk on toward the door but didn't go out before adding, "It wasn't even my fault. They *made* me drink it."

"Right, Elvin," Thor said. "We never heard that one before. And you got pregnant by swimming in the pool with boys, right?"

"Ah, out of Babylon comes young Bishop," Brother Flemming proclaimed as I *eek*ed open the door to the crypt-classroom.

"Oh Jesus," I said, pulling the door closed again.

"Come back here, young man," Flemming commanded.

I returned, reluctantly. After a quick scan of the class I knew that I had reached rock bottom. I had heard about this, the complete moral destruction drinkers suffer when they are finally tapped out. Seeing snakes and rats and mutant creatures with frogs' bodies and Madonna's face. Sleeping with the company of tiny devil-faced, knife-wielding versions of themselves sticking their flesh and laughing all night until they had to jump out of bed and dig up that last bottle of molasses-brown rum in the back-yard and drink it all down like weak tea. Gurgling, gurgling. But I was on the ultra-fast track. I had been a problem drinker for less than twenty-four hours, and already I was surrounded by haunts.

Brother Flemming, head spook. He was here, in this slot of the brotherhood, because he simply could not exist anywhere else. His whole person screamed catechism and Latin Mass, pointer smashes across the knuckles, and you'll go *blind* if you touch that. The little spectacles, the bleached-white head polished to a Turtle Wax sheen on top, fringed with eight or ten foot-long white hairs on the sides. The eyebrows like shaving brushes. Ditto the crops of nose and ear hair. The total absence of any eye move-ment unless he turned his whole head to look at you like the wax-museum version of Vincent Price. The long black dress that most brothers had given up by now but that Flemming wore down past his shoes to give the im-pression of levitating from point to point rather than walking. And then there was his trick of clearing his ever-

busy sinuses by hucking an egg-size lungy into his hand-
kerchief, staring at it mesmerized for a minute as if nobody else was in the room, then folding the hanky neatly
back into his pocket.

His flock wasn't much better. There were only ten of
them, but they were a whole stadium full of weirdness.
The one closest to the door refused to lift his face out of
the Bible on his desk, showing only the vivid bald spot—
ringed with creeping crud—on the top of his head. A
thirteen-year-old kid with a bald spot like Friar Tuck. Behind him were two guys comparing Jesus-head medal-
lions across the aisle, bickering over which one displayed
more anguish. Behind them were two guys who looked
like they must have been brought in in leg chains but who
managed to slip their drug-ravaged structures through the
cuffs. Another guy sitting rigid and smiling with his
hands folded on the desk—*my* idea of a real trouble-
maker. And the rest just appeared to be your run-of-the-
mill scared stiffs like myself who were here seeking the
traditional asylum of the church for the remainder of
camp in hopes of not being wiped out altogether by the
athletic Hun. The sports escapees aren't necessarily hot
for the religion thing but would make a deal with the
devil to bail out of the slot rat race. Since locally god was
more handy, the deal was this.

Not the fourth infantry division we had here, and yet I
was nervous anyway. They were a mob. And any mob
that is not your mob—and *every* mob was not my mob—

is dangerous. Even a mob of wild wimps.

And they had a charismatic leader.

"Here is your Bible, Mr. Bishop. Take it with you to that seat there in back. And that Bible belongs to you for the remainder of the retreat, so you are responsible for it. Take it with you everywhere."

"Everywhere," I said with a little laugh. I had yet to discover that Brother Flemming did not recognize humor when he had committed it.

"Everywhere, sir. That amuses you?"

"Well, ya. As long as you're going to have me haul a Bible around the place with me, why don't you just slap a propeller on my head and paint a big red bull's-eye on my butt? You'll achieve the same thing."

About one third of the class laughed, coincidentally, like hell. One third looked at me and scowled viciously, like You get the stake, I'll get the matches. The final third sank into their seats, looking like Oh god, I hope he doesn't make trouble for *all* of us.

I stopped to appreciate. I liked all of it, all three reactions. I could enjoy this, the only group I was ever in in which I was—The Maverick.

Whack! I never should have taken my eyes off him. He made no sound when he moved.

"*There*'s your propeller, Mr. Bishop." He had clopped me on the ear so hard, I could hear it reddening. "Would you like to further discuss the merits of the Good Book?"

He held the Good Book high overhead. Over *my* head.

"I think I'll just listen for a while," I said.

"See?" Flemming said as he reached for the hanky. "The word of god is already having a positive impact on your life." Then he hucked.

"We here are all on the road to Damascus," Flemming winded from back at his mountaintop desk. "Some of us have already been struck by the power of god's will. *Others* of us"—he turned a fierce stare in my direction—"will need to be struck down off our high horse before we will be ready to change direction."

I felt personally challenged by this guy. He apparently had me set up as his example for the week, but I wasn't going to absorb any hellfire off of *him*, not after all I'd survived already. I raised my hand, almost involuntarily.

"Bishop."

"Um, Brother. I just wanted to say in my defense that, you know, I drank some beer—didn't even enjoy it very much, but that's another story—but anyway, I didn't kill somebody's grandmother or sleep with a sheep."

The reaction, again, was the same breakdown—one third laughs, one third burning stares, one third Leave me out of this. But this time I enjoyed it without taking my eyes off Flemming.

"Ooooo, you got him now." The voice came from over my shoulder. I couldn't see him, but I knew he was one of the laughers. "You struck his pet theme. Bestiality. Makes him crazy."

I smiled, looking right at Flemming as I did.

"You have amused yourself once again, Mr. Bishop?" Flemming growled.

"We take our amusement where we can get it, sir. You understand."

"Uh-oh, watch out," said The Voice. "You've done it again. Favorite theme number two—boys who amuse themselves."

I laughed freely, as if Flemming were in on the joke and would join in any time now.

"I am a patient and forbearing man," Flemming said, beating his pointer into the palm of his free hand like an old-time cop with a nightstick. "But do not test me."

The Voice, from right behind me, would not let me go. "Better stop, Bishop. Don't test him. Whatever you do, don't mention Cub Scouts. For god's sake don't mention Cub Scouts. That was all in the past. They never proved a thing."

"Can I go to the bathroom?" I blurted, spluttering laugh spits all over my desk.

"He was framed, Bishop. He was just walking by that shower stall, and that Cub Scout just happened to slip on the soap, and he accidentally impaled himself on the coincidentally naked brother."

The Voice stopped, and the room was dead silent as I cackled, the way you can only laugh when it's important not to. I held my belly and enjoyed every second. It felt good inside, way beyond eating. This was what was so terrible here at Camp Joyless, I realized. Nobody was into laughing.

Flemming bore down on me. "You are entering one of the finest Christian Brothers schools in America. If you think the study of religion is so funny . . ." His arm came down like he was dropping the checkered flag at the Indy 500. I pulled back, but it was going to split me like a great big log.

Until The Hand shot out. The Hand, belonging to The Voice.

"What do you think you're doing?" Flemming asked with such menace that I got ready for him to try again.

"Ah, I'm stopping a crime," The Voice said, standing now. "You can't do that."

I turned. Attached to a body, The Voice shrank to human scale. He was medium. Medium build, medium complexion, medium height. His actions made him bigger, though. His actions said, simply, "Totally unafraid."

"Oh yes I can do that," Flemming said.

Before the two of them got into an embarrassing duke-out over me, I intervened.

"Thanks," I said to my protector, then stood to face the brother myself. "No, really, you can't do that."

"And why not?"

"Well, because I can't let you. See, it's like this: First there was the whole shanghai thing that got me here in the first place . . . then the football stompings, the baseball beanings . . . Jesus, the mole business, the humiliation . . . wrestling, running, not wrestling . . . and none of that did me in. I'm not broken, you see? So if I let myself be broken by one little guy with a big stick . . . well, you can see how that would mean it was all for nothing. So, brother, no, I can't let you do that."

"So suck on *that*," The Voice cheered.

Flemming stared at me, dumbstruck, as if I was speaking in tongues. Maybe no other victim had ever tried to explain himself before. So he turned to The Voice instead. "Get out," he said.

"Psyched," The Voice answered. "New record, thirty minutes. I lasted in track and field a whole day."

He brushed past Flemming, who had lost interest in me. The Brother went back to the front of the class and started firing up his brimstone again. "Get thee behind me, Satan," he said, making a stiff-arm gesture at the exiting Voice.

"Fine," The Voice answered. "Just as long as thee don't get behind *me*."

Again, I had that feeling of being alone in the audience of a comedy no one else was hearing. It wasn't that I had anything necessarily against god—other than his sense of humor, which I didn't share—or Flemming personally. It was just that I had had enough. I didn't want to be bullied or instructed or improved in any way. I wanted a laugh. And I wasn't scared of anything anymore, except the fear that I might never laugh again.

"Is that it?" I said, pointing at The Voice, who had stopped in the doorway. "That's all he had to do, up and leave?"

The Voice started beckoning me to do it too.

"Shall I drive you someplace?" replied the totally disgusted Brother, pointing me to the door with his pointer. "Call you a cab, perhaps?"

I got up and walked toward the door, moving slowly,

waiting for the catch. There was none, though. However, I did notice a strange thing in people's eyes. Something like respect.

The most outrageous thing yet. They thought I was cool here. I was not a geek in this room, I was a hellion. I almost wanted to stay.

"You missed a great opportunity here, Bishop," Flemming said triumphantly. "Your mother will now be informed of your transgression."

"Well my mother already *knows* about the sheep. And she loves me anyway."

I think even some of the religious geeky kids were snickering when I left.

"The name is Oskar, and I'm sorry I got you in trouble. Nah, never mind. I'm not sorry. You needed salvation from there, and I salvated you. And it's Oskar with a K, the German one, not the baloney one with a C."

Oskar walked along in way-too-big dungarees flopping over his sneakers, which was the style, and a way-too-small sweatshirt, which was not. Fine black hair kept draping down over one eye, and he kept brushing it back.

"Okay, Oskar, where are we walking to?"

"Our new assignment."

"How do we have a new assignment already?"

"End of the line. Last-Chance Saloon. Bottom rung. The dregs. Underside of the rock. The Slot of Last Resort. Home."

"How do you know already?"

"I'm a veteran. Second-year freshman. They figure as

long as I am repeating the year, they might as well have me repeat the stupid damn camp too. Take another shot at reforming me, you see. Hah!"

He walked like a German Oskar. Fast, direct, sure of where he was going. I struggled to keep up.

"Fat chance they had at that," he said proudly. "Same script as last year. Football, baseball, track, hockey, religion, then splash, hit bottom. I couldn't wait."

"But that's you. Maybe they'll have another plan for me. I should go back to Thor, just to check. They might not let me in."

"Hah!" he said again. Oskar seemed fond of getting to the point. He took a long look at me, up and down, as he kept marching. *"First,"* he barked, holding up one finger, "they have to take you here. Nobody gets turned away. *Second"*—he held up the second finger now, making a rather aggressive peace sign—"you belong. You'll love it."

Suddenly, we were there. "Here?" I asked, a great stretch of a grin opening on my face. He nodded and winked. We took the stairs two at a time. Well, he did. I took them two, then one, then two, then one.

At the front door Oskar turned the knob briskly, then kicked it open, making enough racket to attract the attention of everyone in the room. All eyes turned to us, and I found myself staring back. It was as if somebody had thrown on a light in some secret experimental geek lab in the middle of the night where the mad scientist was building a separate race out of mismatched and discarded pieces of all the other slots.

"Welcome to the Arts Sector," Oskar laughed.

"In the library," I said, the smile holding steady.

Mother Superior,

    Would that thou mightst have witnessed the greatest yet accomplishment of thy sole progeny.

    They kicked me out of Religion Sector.

    It was a classic clash of power. I was like Martin Luther, throwing open the floor to new ideas, winning converts left and right, only to be excommunicated for it. Half the class was lining up to join my sect when they ran me out of there.

    But they cannot contain it now. Elvinism is coming.

Yours in Christ,
Bishop Elvin

Chapter 11

Through the cracks of society.

When I got up that next morning, I didn't stumble blindly into my old workout routine. I still woke before everybody else, but this time I just lay there, knowing I didn't have to get my body in shape for anything. I lay there staring, listening to the breathing of the animals all around me inside and the chirps of the animals outside. I thought about the impossible geekdom of the Arts Sector and laughed, wondering what I was possibly going to do over there. I rustled, adjusted my pillow, closed my eyes, pretending to myself that I wanted to enjoy some more lazy sleep. Then I did what I really wanted to do. I got up, dressed, stretched, feeling my muscles screaming yet alive again. Then I went out and ran. Just because I felt like it.

I started sweating the instant I stepped out the door. It felt good. I jogged, I strode, I ran. I stroked it. Fluid, right arm up, left knee up, left arm up, right leg up. Two breaths up, two down. All my parts were working together, like they knew what they were doing, like they knew each other well. It hurt, of course. It was hard, of course. I was still tortoise slow, of course. But I was in sync, and I was enjoying it. I was better, running down the road, down the path, amid the trees, up the hill, than I had ever been before. Because I took a day off? Why didn't I think of that before, to just take a day off to recharge?

Because I was an athlete before. An organized athlete. A slottist. And they don't do that. They don't take days off, ever.

Now I could enjoy it, and I did. I felt stronger, freer, more efficient. Better. Because I was doing it for nothing and nobody. I ran and ran harder, pushed myself, panted, felt the heartburn and the charley horse burn. I almost wished I *did* have football players to smash into later that day, almost wished I *did* have wrestlers to break.

I laughed as I ran up the hill—no small effort to do those two together. I remembered I'd need all my strength to slay the wild arts horde.

I was very nearly to the top of the hill when I caught myself. I stopped dead before reaching the peak. The campsite. I didn't want to see that. Whatever it was like now, I didn't want to see it. I turned around and rumbled back down.

There were a hundred million differences, give or take a mil, between the Arts Sector and all the others. Starting right at the top, the Brothers. While all the sports slots had one or two official Brothers hanging around drinking iced tea and clapping just to make the "non-sports" camp look legit while lay coaches did all the real work, Arts Sector was crawling with Brothers. Busy Brothers. And while the Brothers who did nothing everywhere else went out of their way to look Brotherly—the black suit, shoes, socks, half-white collar even in the blistering sun—you couldn't tell that the Arts Brothers were Brothers unless they told you. The largest swatch of black in the whole library—other than on the students, who were dripping in it—was Brother Clarke's cloud of fuzzy black hair. It was about a foot high off his head—like Larry of the Three Stooges if he wasn't balding.

I met Brother Clarke first, the instant I entered the library. It smelled wonderful, and he was the reason why.

"Drink?" he asked, still hunched over a small hissing black machine on a table.

"What?"

"Drink, I said. Or, rather, Drink? with a question mark. As in, Do you? Would you? Like a drink? Café? Espresso?"

I dumbfounded him with my dumbfounded expression.

Brother Clarke gently put his cup down on the table, then not-so-gently grabbed my shoulders and shook me. "Coffee. Coffee, boy. For god's sake, don't you smell it?

Are you with us, son?" Even after he stopped talking, he kept shaking me.

"No-o-o," I burbled. "None-for-me-thanks. And-you-might-think-about-cutting-down-yourself."

He laughed, gave me one last good shake, and pinched my cheek. "So, what do you do?" he asked, challenged, really, but in a funnish, robust way. He swiped up his mug with one hand and put the other hand in his pocket, waiting for an answer. When I hesitated, he dramatically looked at his watch.

"What do you mean, what do I do? Like, do I have a job?"

Brother Clarke blinked at me fifty times, shifted his weight back and forth and back and forth as if waiting for me to answer was like waiting in a long bathroom line.

"Artistically speaking," he said finally. "What is your gift?"

"Oh, that," I said, nodding and pointing my I-get-it finger at him. "None."

"I see, no gift. What, then, is your strength?"

"Okay," I said, nodding some more, "now we're getting somewhere. My strength? None."

"I see, no strength. How about . . . er, proclivity? You got a proclivity?"

"Nope."

"Leaning?"

"Straight up and down."

"Inclination?"

201

"Without."

"Aptitude?"

"Getting colder."

Brother Clarke let out a great sigh, refilled his coffee, and asked with his back to me, "Have you got any ambition at all?"

"Yes," I said surely. "I want to go home."

"*Finally*," he proclaimed, throwing his coffee-free hand up into the air, "we're getting somewhere. Tap your ruby slippers together and follow me."

I followed along as Brother Clarke led me through the library. It was a different place now from the building that had belonged to only me the week before. The lights were all on. Here and there guys were slumped at tables, reading, painting, or doing projects that were unfathomable to me, making god knows what out of god knows what. One guy was making a model out of what looked like mud, building, I think, a Madonna except she kept disintegrating because the mix was too watery.

"What is your name?" Brother Clarke asked over his shoulder.

"Bishop," I said. "Elvin Bishop."

"Bishop Elvin Bishop. It's dramatic. Like Ford Maddox Ford, right? Or William Carlos Williams. Or Flavor Flav. What do you want to be called? Bishop? Elvin? Bishy?"

"Elvin," I said, stopping to do a double take as a guy stroked a coat of shellac over what I swore were dog droppings. After a few seconds the guy felt my presence.

"Gonna be a napkin holder. For my mom," he said icily.

"You haven't been deloused yet, have you, Bishy?"

"Elvin."

"Come on, you can't tell me you got through over two weeks of sports camp without being nicknamed."

"Big Booty," I sighed.

"Good one," Brother Clarke said.

"And if you were at the talent show, you may remember me as The Masked Potato."

"No way. You were The Potato? Hot damn."

"Ya, I'm kind of a celeb. Free Willy, The White Tornado, Squishy Bishy . . ."

"Ouch. Free Willy, huh? Is that because you're heavy, or because you're boring?"

I stared at him deadly.

"We'll go with your regular name then. Okay, Elvin, let's get you deloused."

"Let's," I said, though I had no idea what he was talking about.

He threw open the door to the periodicals room, where a meeting was in progress. Brother Clarke shoved me down into a seat at the back of the room as a student stood to speak. It took the kid a long while to stand all the way up to his full elongated height, but when he did, I brightened.

"My name is Paul Burman," he said sadly, tentatively, "and I hate the shit out of basketball. I spent the last two weeks taking passes in the pivot from some psychopath who would not let me alone. They were so hot to have my body in the slot that they wouldn't let me out until I took off all my clothes in the middle of a scrimmage and played naked for five minutes. I blocked three shots with my privates dangling."

There was polite applause all around.

"My name is Lennox," the next outcast said. "I was a prisoner of wrestling for two weeks. I want to paint."

"I want to sculpt."

"I want to draw."

"I want to build."

"My name is Eugene, and I *do* bathe, twice a day. And I don't have to be here. And when school starts I will be back on the wrestling team, but I want to do other things. I want to sing."

I knew them. I knew every one of them. I hadn't been slotted with every single one of them, but I knew each one, somehow. We'd sat at adjoining tables at mealtimes, or crossed paths while being ejected from one slot or another, or logged some time together in sick bay. There wasn't a guy in here who hadn't nodded his head or said "hey" or "how ya doin'" to me as we floated by on our paths to very different places. The football players didn't do that. If I didn't keep my head up and jump out of the way, they'd trample me rather than say "hi" or "excuse me." My own Cluster mates would go days without acknowledging me or half of their other neighbors. But all these guys . . .

What was I doing here with all these geeks?

And where did they get all this focus? Half of them couldn't tell you what month it was out there in the real world, or if they needed a drink of water, but suddenly, here, they had the answer. "I want to be a dancer. I want to be an architect . . ." Where did all this come from?

"You, sir," Brother Fox said, pointing to me.

"Me, sir?" I repeated, also pointing to me.

"You, sir."

Brother Clarke nudged me, and I got up. Nervously, I spit it out. "I started in football. Then I got knocked out and went to sick bay. Then I went to baseball. Then I went to sick bay. Then I spent a long time in wrestling, a little more time in sick bay . . . then I golfed, which put me *really* in sick bay; then I got Religion Sector."

That brought the big reaction. When I bottomed out with the Religion Sector, the heartfelt moans that were directed my way—even from the Brothers—even made *me* get all choked up for the poor sap we were discussing, whoever he was. Heads shook, the hands were raised to cover mouths, as if what I'd really said was "and *then* the big one held me while the little one pistol whipped me. And *then* . . ." We were all on the brink of tears.

"It's been a long road, hasn't it, son?" Brother Fox said. "What is your name?"

"Bishop, Brother."

"Well, Bishy—"

Brother Clarke started waving his arms at Brother Fox. "Ix-nay on the ishy-Bay," he said, kindly.

"Well, Mr. Bishop," Brother Fox said, pausing for emphasis and looking all around the room to include all the sad sacks. "That shit's history. You're artists now."

There was a round of laughs and applause as everyone stood.

"Whoever wants to do performance, drama, music, follow Brother Crudelle that way," he announced, and three guys walked out behind the Brother who looked like Jesus only skinnier. "Those of you who want to try painting, drawing, sculpting, or other visual arts, go with Brother Mattus." Half the group got up and followed after Mattus, who looked like a cross between Santa Claus and Rasputin. "Those of you interested in exploring printmaking, textile art, mixed media, abstract art, experimental art, and the study of art history will be coming with me." There were six of us left, obviously the six who had no idea what we wanted and were waiting to be struck by something. "And the last group, going with Brother Percy, will be those interested in poetry and prose."

Well that decided it. The other five fence sitters hurried to line up behind Brother Fox.

Myself, I remained. Like the moment before, and the year before. Undecided. Unclear. Unmoved. Unattracted. Paralyzed with the depth of my own nothingness. I made my decision the way I made all my decisions. By sitting passively.

Brother Percy walked up to me, chuckling. The last of the last were filing out of the room as he sat backward on the chair in front of me. "You don't know it yet," he said, "but we are an elite class, you and I. After sifting and sifting, weeding and sorting, picking and cleaning, and sifting again, out of the bottom of the sieve drops only the finest grain of all."

I looked at him, leaning closer, to try and see if he was for real. I couldn't tell.

"The dregs, you mean," I said.

He stood up over me, a medium-built six one, with prematurely silver collarbone-length hair. "Son," he said with a generous face, extending a hand for me to shake, "I perceive in you a problem of perspective."

I shook his hand and he tugged me up out of the chair.

"What if I *hate* poetry?" I asked as he led me out with his arm around my shoulders. I figured I'd break it to him in stages that I did, in fact, hate poetry already.

"Then you move on," he said, shrugging. "You are not tied to any one art while you're here. Everyone is welcome to float from one area to another if he likes, and every year most of the fellows do. In fact, I insist you do."

"What if I don't *want* to?" I snapped, out of reflex. My wick was burning down quickly in the last days of camp.

"Ah, a bona fide contrarian. This is going to be a pleasure. A *pleasure*," he said.

"But look at them," I said, making a sweeping gesture with my hand over the main room of the library. It was already abuzz with eager rookie artists making a lunatic formless cheery colorful mess of the place. Santa's workshop merged with *One Flew Over the Cuckoo's Nest*. "They're all geeks. They're all mental."

Brother Percy took it as a compliment. He inhaled deeply, as if he could breathe all the mentalness in. "Yes," he said. "Aren't we?"

Mama,
    Whole new me, volume eighty-seven.
        There once was a boy from Massachusetts
        Whose mother thought him dumb fat and useless
        So she threw him a bone
        Ninety miles from his home
        And today he was slotted with the fruitses.

                            Yours,
                            Elvin, Lord Bishop

When I showed up the next morning, the first person I saw was Oskar. Because he was doing his work outside on the lawn.

"Steee-rike!" he yelled after nailing a three-by-three-foot cardboard square with a glob of paint. "Elvin," he called happily when he saw me. He stretched both hands to the hazy white sky in greeting. It looked like he was wearing psychedelic gloves, paint coating his hands and halfway up his forearms. "Congratulate me—I did it. I got ejected from the previously unejectable Arts Sector. *God*, I'm a man," he said, scooping a handful of black from a jar and slinging it.

"You didn't," I said.

"Nah, not really. Partway, though. I was making such

208

a mess, they asked me to take it outside. I can go back in when I'm done."

I looked around. There was not a brush anywhere near him. He was exclusively throwing paint at his canvas. And having a ball.

"Yar!" he said. "A little titanium white there. Yar! A bit of vermilion up there."

"Looks like fun, Oskar. Can I have a throw?"

He turned on me darkly, stopping his fun for a minute. "What do you think, this is a joke? This is no game, this is a work of art I'm doing here. I can't let you just come in and screw it up."

I stared at the work. "Oh. Sorry."

"Don't mention it," he said, returning to his work, and to his bright mood. "Indigo!" he called. *Splatch.*

"Um, what is it?" I asked, half ducking in anticipation.

"You don't know?"

I shook my head.

"Come on, Elvin, it's right there. It's our class picture. It's us." He rushed up to the portrait, pointed excitedly to a gob of green half on, half drooping off, the lower right-hand corner. "That's you."

I don't know what happened to me there—maybe it was Oskar's intensity, or his pride and enjoyment of it all, but I saw it. It looked like me. It looked like all of us.

"I like it," I said. "Except I have a little more hair than that, and I part it on the other side."

He held up his dripping hands as if to stop me. "Sorry, man. That's my vision."

I left him with his vision. I went inside.

"Drink?" Brother Clarke said cheerfully, hunched over his espresso machine again.

"No, thank you," I said, walking on past toward the busy crafts table. Just as I got there, three guys plunked their faces down into bowls of puttylike goop. Three other guys pushed the heads down deeper from behind, held them there, then helped them back out. I crept closer to check it out as they toweled off, and saw perfect impressions of their faces in the bowls.

"Beautiful," Brother Fox crowed, clapping. "Then we'll pour liquid into this mold to make the mask. And when that is hardened, you can paint it or do whatever you like, to make it look however you want it to look."

"Cool," I said, not meaning to say it to anyone but me.

"Come on over, Elvin," Lennox said. "Do one."

I was already backing away. "Nah, I'm just looking," I said.

I backed into Brother Percy. "Morning, Elvin," he said. "You ready to do some work?"

Now I backed in the other direction. "Um, no. I thought I'd float for a while. You know, investigate other stuff."

"Bravo," he said, and walked away just like that.

The music was hard to ignore. It was also hard to like. Anyhow, it drew me down to the farthest end of the library, under the short balcony that ran the width of the building with stairs at either end. The door to the conservatory was ajar, so I nudged it, not really accidentally.

Brother Crudelle was seated at an upright piano, wearing a starched white short-sleeved shirt buttoned to the collar, but still looking cool crisp white. Opposite him, leaning on the top of the tall piano with their elbows, were the two giants. Eugene and Paul Burman. Singing.

Sort of. They didn't sound good. They didn't blend. They weren't singing words, only sounds to match whatever chord Crudelle hit. They sounded like old cars, with the springs gone and many small holes in the mufflers.

But as far as I could tell, they didn't know it. They were up on their toes, both of them, as if they needed it, trying to reach notes that would bring the rest of us to our knees. When Eugene saw me, his glossy face beamed, and he made a "yo" fist power sign. Paul couldn't see me because he had his eyes shut tight.

When I first followed that sound, I was hoping it would be good for a laugh. But when I got there, it was a whole different show. I left the room and closed the door quietly. I sat down on the steps with my chin on my fist. This was a better place, I could already tell, because everyone here seemed so comfortable. But they were gripping something I wasn't quite gripping. I mean, I was happier here, but I was no less confused.

"Ready?" Brother Percy said, calling down to me from the balcony at the top of the stairs.

"No," I said.

"Start with this," he said, dangling a book between his thumb and index finger. When it was obvious that I was looking at it, he let it drop, and I caught it.

It was *Selected Writings of Edgar Allan Poe*. I looked at

it for a few seconds, didn't open it, then threw it back up.

"Listen, you," I said boldly. "I hate this stuff. I hate poetry. I hate Edgar Allan Poe except for the detective stories. The horror stuff is about half as scary as Barney the Dinosaur. I saw all the movies with Vincent Price. They were hysterical. I read 'The Raven' a hundred times in school, and it got more boring every time. Nevermore, already."

He didn't speak. He smirked like he knew everything. Then he dropped a second book. *The Poetry of Robert Frost*.

"Car commercials," I snapped, and threw it back.

The third book dropped, and Brother Percy's smile along with it. It was a paperback with a bright-pink cover. *Final Harvest*, poems by Emily Dickinson.

"I think I'm going to try clay modeling today," I said, and tossed the book back. He refused to catch this one. It rose, arced, then fell back to me.

"Fine, but hold on to that one anyway. It'll fit in your back pocket, and you can read it when you feel like it."

This seemed like a good escape point, so I gave in. Even though he was exaggerating a bit—good thing I have large back pockets. I stashed the book and made busy, spending most of my time just poking around, looking at other people's work, watching, feeling the textures of what everybody else was working, the clay, the paint, the piano keys, the soft metal, the wet paper. Watching it all from over shoulders.

Once, just after lunch, when nobody was looking, I

picked up a brush and tried to make a picture. Of a house, and a small car, and a road and two people. When the painters returned, I crumpled mine up and threw it in the trash, burrowing to get it underneath the other trash.

"What is *that*?" Frankie demanded as he walked up behind me at Nightmeal. He pulled the book out of my pocket and took it with him to the other side of the table.

"It's a book, ape boy. Give it back."

He stared at it in his hands as if it was a talking severed head. "El, it's a *poetry* book. It's a *pink* poetry book."

I made a stab to get it back, but Frankie was too fast. Then, quick as a cobra, Mikie snatched it and gave it to me.

"God, this is the worst slot yet, Elvin," Frank said, real concern on his face. "How are we gonna get you out of this one?"

"I'll be fine," I said. "Don't help me anymore."

Mike extended his palm. He wanted to have another look at the book. "You really into poetry, El?" he said, browsing as he talked.

"NO," I insisted. "That's just what I backed into. Now I have this poetry teacher who has absolutely nothing to do except follow me around, haunting me with this stuff. He's got *nobody* but me."

"Do you have to stay?" Mike asked.

"No. Everybody's pretty free over there."

"So move, then."

"Ya, Jesus, move out of there for god's sake," Frank said. "That stuff's got nothing to do with you."

"Move to where?" I asked. I asked Mike, not Frank.

"Good question," Frank answered. "That whole Arts Sector gives me the creeps. All the weird guys are there."

Mike and I banded together to try to ignore him. "Well is there something else you want to do? Like do you want to paint or something?"

"No. I don't know. Ya. I don't know."

"That's good, Elvin," Frank jumped in. "Things are clearing up nicely now."

"Okay, so here's what I'm doing. I'm watching. I'm watching a couple of guys mixing paints together, and you wouldn't believe it. They combine this kind of yellow, that I've seen somewhere before, and that kind of blue, which I've seen before, and they mix and mix, and add a drop and another drop, and they come up with a green I have *never* seen before. Mike, I watched paint mixing for an hour and a half. And all this one guy did when he got the color just right was he painted a circle, like a moon or a planet or something near the top of his canvas. Then he went on and mixed something else."

Frank said nothing, just stared at me like I was retarded. Mike said nothing. But he stared and waited for the *more* of it.

"But I felt like I *did* something there. Like I had *been* someplace. Seeing what they did, being there for it, hanging over their shoulders, was like, so satisfying. So I tried it.

214

The kid saw me hovering, offered me a brush, and I tried."

Mike thought this was the big discovery part of the story. "There we go," he said.

"No, there we *don't* go," I said. "I hated it. I painted with watercolors for ten minutes, then went crazy and threw a glass of water all over what I'd done."

"You're getting really *weird*, Elvin," Frank said, looking at me sideways.

"So painting wasn't for you." Mikie shrugged.

"No, it wasn't." I said, banging my fist on my supper tray "And neither was music or pottery or collage. All that was for me was *watching*. Watching. Watching and watching. Mikie. I found out, that's all I really want to do. But when I'm doing the watching, I feel like I'm doing the *doing*. You know? I mean, it's much better than when I do it myself."

"We have to get you fixed, El," Frankie said, drop-dead serious now. "I don't like the way you're sounding. You're not your old self."

I thought I wasn't listening to Frank, but he was getting to me anyhow. I leaned more desperately toward Mikie, who had the ignoring Frank thing locked. "Is that all right?" I asked. "Can I do that? Is something wrong with me? Is that a slot a person can have? Watcher?"

"Does anyone mind, that you're doing all the watching?"

"No. I think they like it, even, having an audience."

"Then it should be fine."

"Ya. I suppose. Except that poetry guy. He seems to think I should be doing something."

"We have to get you straight," Frank repeated, shaking his head slowly. "Listen. Last night of camp, this Saturday, Obie and the guys are having a send-off party. Gonna be a big blast. Now this time, you guys are *not* invited, because of your awful behavior in the past, but I bet I could get you in, seeing as I'm like the guest of honor and all."

"No, thank you," I said quickly. "Actually, the Arts Sector is having its own little party Saturday night in the library."

"What do you mean, the guest of honor?" Mike finally addressed Frank.

"My debut party. My coming-out party. Passing of the torch stuff. I told you guys this from the beginning. I told you these guys were the people to know. Now they're handing the keys over to me, making me the new king. Like I said, they're leaving, I'm coming in. Changing of the guard. I'm going to be king. But don't worry, I won't forget you guys."

Frank grinned. He had been waiting a long time to make that speech, or one just like it. Mikie went stone cold again. I was—no surprise—confused. I was happy for Frank, because Frank was happy for himself and that didn't happen as often as most people thought. But I was afraid too. I didn't think I wanted him to be King of All the Wild Things.

"So they're having a party, your whole Sector?" Mike

asked, shutting Frank's story off.

"Ya," I said. "Goofy, huh? They're all really weird, Mike."

"Basketball Sector's just going to show a highlight film of the Knicks-Rockets finals. Even big hoops fans don't want to look at *that*."

"Yuck." Frank and I finally agreed on something.

"And you're allowed to do pretty much whatever you want?" Mike went on.

"Pretty much," I said.

"Cool," Mikie said.

"Cool?" Frank said. "Please, Mike, we only have a few days left here. We need at least *you* to come out of it the same as when you came in."

Chapter 12

Coronations and crossroads.

I sat at a table early the next morning, watching the only other guy in the place. I was the second person here, as I was getting up earlier each day now, running and showering and eating faster than I had before. This guy, though, was always here. He was here at night when the last of us went to get Nightmeal, and he was here no matter what time we got here in the morning.

He liked glass. He was always doing things with glass. His dark face pressed right up against whatever he was working on, squinting hard through his own glasses, which were two fingers thick.

This morning he was cutting—cutting a green, then a brown, then a clear, then a black bottle into strips like long glass French fries, with a glass cutter. There wasn't a sound yet in the building other than the *scratch-chink*ing of the tool ripping the glass. Then he super-glued a piece of fishing line to the top of each, carefully cutting very specific different lengths and assigning each to just the right shard. When he had them all assembled into the mobile, he picked it up and held it high above his head for us both to examine.

The sun from a high window shot down through it and shattered into shafts and shadows of those four colors plus four more and four more. He blew lightly on it and it tinkled nicely, but the music was half what the light show was. He turned to me, allowing himself the faintest smile.

"What do you see?" he asked.

I was absolutely certain.

"I see fifty pairs of hands, made of ice, flying straight down wiggling their fingers, trying to reach something and touch it."

He looked away from me, back up at his thing. Then he looked back at me again. "That's right," he said, and went off to hang it from the sash of that window.

"Drink?" Brother Clarke called out.

I hadn't even noticed when he came in. "No, thanks," I said. The glass kid didn't answer, just dug out his soldering iron from a fishing-tackle box of art supplies and went to work on a lead frame for a window he was making.

Since not much else was happening yet, I sat at a corner table and read some of my book so that I'd have something to say to Brother Percy. I read the introduction about Emily Dickinson and how she never, ever left home and how she didn't want to see anybody or make new friends or, basically, do anything. I *hated* it. I shut the book when I got to the first two lines of the first example:

> *The Soul selects her own Society—*
> *Then—Shuts the Door—*

"Ready to work?" Brother Percy said, sneaking up from behind and clapping me on the shoulder.

"Here," I said, shoving the book back into his hands. "I hate poetry. And I'm *not* nuts."

"Mercurial, that's good. You've got the tempera-ment . . ."

I was about to yell at him to get away when there was a loud smack against the window nearest us. We both turned to look.

"What was that?" I asked.

He pointed casually at the substance running down the pane. "An egg," he sighed. "Don't worry about it. You'll learn to ignore it."

"Faggots," a gravelly voice called from outside. A second egg hit, and another on the next window. Then the sound of several people running away.

"So you don't care for Emily Dickinson?" Brother Percy asked, right back to business.

"Huh?" I was still staring up at the window.

"You want a new book."

"Um, ya. That doesn't bother you?" I said, pointing up at the egged window bubbling in the sun.

"Of course it bothers me. If I could do anything about it, I would. But since I couldn't do anything about it last year or the year before or the year before, I figure it's best to just go on with our work."

"Well couldn't you at least tell somebody? So they know?"

"Tell somebody? Like whom?"

"I don't know. Like, the boss. Brother Jackson."

Brother Percy covered his laugh with his hand. Then he turned out to the room at large, where all the other artist Brothers were busy ignoring the eggs and trying to teach their students to do likewise. "Hey," Brother Percy called out, "Elvin wants to know why we just don't go tell Brother Jackson what happened."

They all laughed together, a nasty angry laugh that wasn't aimed at me exactly, but at the situation.

"Good idea, Elvin," Brother Mattus, the Santa Claus, bellowed. "But you better run and catch him right now before he washes his hands."

It was scary, the way the Brothers all laughed together at that.

"Fine," Brother Percy said, returning to the subject and finally seeming to get a little agitated with me. He snatched the book up.

I snatched the book back. Frankie was right: I was getting weird. "I'll just hold on to it until you find another one for me."

"Deal," Brother Percy said, and he went back to browsing the stacks.

I felt guilty. He was trying so hard. I just had no poetry in me, and no interest. But I tried, to make him feel better. I opened the book to the middle and read some more.

I winced, shut the book again. "You're no Rummy Macias, Emily," I said. "God, I *hate* poetry."

"Then quit it," Mikie said.

I looked up and he was standing there.

"You made it sound so good," he said, grinning.

The rest of the week was fun, with me and Mikie finally together again, and for the most part it was quiet. I brought him around to show him the ropes of watching other artists work. But that wasn't good enough. He wanted to do stuff. So he did. He painted a little. He sculpted a clay dog modeled after the late Freckles, his old Scottie. He remembered enough of his piano lessons to nudge Brother Crudelle off the stool and play for a while. He drank Brother Clarke's espresso, which made Brother Clarke very happy. He did a little of this and a little of that, and as usual he was pretty good at everything although not great at any one thing. And as usual he was a hit and everyone liked him and he fit like a glove.

But not as usual, I wasn't jealous of him. He had a good time, and I had a good time watching him do it. Just like I had a good time watching all the other artists do their thing.

Brother Percy kept bringing me books and I kept rejecting them. It got kind of fun for both of us. I am no poet.

We kept getting egged. We kept getting screamed at and laughed at, and usually the windows looked like there was some kind of grotesque storm going on outside even though it was sunny every day. It was all supposed to be just a joke.

By the end of the week, people had settled down to their final projects, to be unveiled at the party Saturday night. Thursday and Friday were the quietest, with groups broken off into corners to do their hush-hush work. I was the only one who was allowed to look at everybody's work. They guarded it all jealously from each other, but they all let me see.

Friday, as we were clearing out, Brother Percy stepped up to me. It occurred to me that he hadn't forced a book on me for over twenty-four hours. I thought he'd quit. He looked tired.

"You nearly wore me out, Elvin," he said. "I've been watching you. I've been studying you for clues."

"That must have been a thrill," I said, laughing. "I haven't been doing *anything*."

"Yes you have," he said, giving me the smarty smile I thought I had killed three days ago. He marched past me to the back of the library, under the balcony, to the far corner, where he disappeared briefly into the shadows. Then he came back out, retraced his steps, stood before me, and held out the book. It was a skinny little paperback, *Winesburg, Ohio*, by Sherwood Anderson. I flipped through it, just to be polite.

"This isn't poetry," I said.

"Maybe it is, maybe it isn't," he answered.

I ignored the book. It sat in my back pocket like the

rest, until I went to bed. Then I saw it again when I stripped and it fell on the floor. It looked like a challenge this time. I picked it up and hit the bed, determined to give this last one a look if only to show Brother Percy that no matter how much he watched me, watched me watching, he didn't know me.

I opened the book. When I read the name of the first chapter, "The Book of Grotesques," in which the narrator talks about everybody he ever knew, about everybody in the world, as somehow deformed and wrong, I knew I was going to read more.

"Grotesques," I thought. "I get it now. It's not me after all. It's everybody else."

And when I saw the chapter "Mother," I jumped ahead, for personal reasons. And when the boy said to his mother, "There isn't any use. I don't know what I shall do. I just want to go away and look at people and think," I didn't wonder anymore why I was reading this. I stayed up as long as I could that night, reading the story of the boy who did nothing but watch people and think. And who grew up while he did it.

I woke up Saturday morning with the book across my face. I lifted it and finished reading. Then I did my stuff, my run and all, in the quiet of the second-to-last morning. Saturday was a funky nowhere day. The breakup stuff was happening that night, and we were all going home tomorrow, but the day was free.

I went to the library, and it was nice to have it back to myself. I cleared my little space at the librarian's desk, turned on that one dim desk lamp, and pulled out the pencil and paper.

"Last chance, Elvin. Sure you won't come?" Frankie stood combing his long curly hair in the bathroom mirror, bouncing to some music I couldn't hear. He was fired up. "It's going to be the blowout of your life," he said. "I know you don't want to miss this."

"I don't think I'm ready yet for the blowout of my life," I answered. "I figure I've got a couple of years left. You do it for me."

"Okay, I will. Then next time, when I'm in charge, maybe you'll come to the parties with me." He patted my belly as he passed by me in the doorway. Then he was out. I watched him running to get where he was going.

We'd been told to skip Nightmeal and come directly to the library, so I met Mikie at his Cluster and we hiked on down together.

"Frankie's gone already?" Mike asked.

"He is."

That was the whole conversation. All Mike could do these days was shake his head about Frankie and his friends. I thought he was taking it all too seriously. Being too much Dad. But he couldn't help that.

"Drink?" Brother Clarke urged us both as we came in. "Come on, now, you have to drink." He gestured around the room where everybody apparently was drinking his espresso. He leaned closer. "It's only decaf. And just for tonight, I'm allowing milk and sugar."

225

We took our cups and pushed on into the party. And to my surprise it was a real party. The Arts Brothers had gotten together a nice spread, set up over a long conference table, of crustless sandwiches, tuna, turkey, ham and Swiss. Bowls with two kinds of olives. I hate olives, but they looked great. Brownies, lemonade, Coke, tortilla chips, salsa, guacamole, blue cheese dip. There was even a green salad and a potato salad. All the young artists were bent over the food table, working their plastic plates like palettes as they piled up. It was the first meal in three weeks that wasn't some industrially produced unnatural form pressed out of the chopped and filled and reconstituted form of something that was once an actual foodstuff combined with many things that were not.

I squeezed in next to Oskar, the mad paint mixer. "You know what color that is?" he asked me excitedly, pointing at one of the bowls of olives. "It's *olive*," he said, thrilled.

We sat on chairs, on floors, on stairs, as we took our food cookout style to wherever we liked. Mike followed me up the stairs, where we took the balcony, overlooking everybody else.

A sound came from somewhere. From a black rectangular tape recorder like the ones they use in the schools to go along with fifty-year-old slide shows on the building of the Grand Coulee Dam. What was coming out of it now, though, was music. It was awfully tinny, like the orchestra was playing through a megaphone, and it was some expired classical stuff to boot. But it was music. I realized that—besides the practice-room exercises with the library piano, which *hardly* counted—this was the first shred of music I'd heard since I'd been here. It was welcome. Boring, but most definitely welcome.

"Ah, *The Magic Flute*." Brother Crudelle hummed, closing his eyes and conducting the imaginary orchestra. Maybe he could get them to play better.

"Ah," everybody replied. But we were mostly just being nice.

Something hung from the light fixture in the middle of the room. It was the size of a big person, wrapped in a blanket, tied and hanging eight feet off the floor.

Artwork hung on a wall, draped in black cloth. One easel stood in the corner, another in the middle of the room. A long table, draped completely in black, had bumps poking up all over it.

How had they done all this in such a short time? I was in the library all day until just a couple of hours ago.

The first to present his project, while we were all still munching desert, was Oskar. With a dramatic *swoosh* he ripped the cover from his canvas, the one in the middle of the room. It was his group portrait of us. He stood next to it, beaming, checking us all out for our reactions. As if we hadn't all seen it already. It was the same and only thing he'd worked on all week, on the lawn, in full view.

"But it's *so* different now," he said. "Look, there's Brother Mattus, the big brown part, Brother Fox over there . . ."

"Ah" was the general reaction, and the theme of the evening. Oskar received his round of quiet golf-gallery applause graciously.

We moved, as one floating mass, on to the wall, where the drape was removed to reveal the three masks, decorated now with each artist/subject's own version of himself. One guy had added a layer of clay in the form of a goalie mask to his face, topping that with black-painted scar stitches all over. The next had added a nose ring, war paint, and a white goat-beard three feet long. The last, Lennox, with the round face, had painted his a brilliant starch white, adding plum lipstick and a thin black line ringing each eye. Lennox, the other fat guy, who'd coached me into pinning him so that we could both be done with wrestling. Lennox, it turned out, was a beauty.

We took a break, ate some more, and started to like the music. The crazy art-glass kid couldn't help himself, dug out some materials, and got to work on his stained-glass window.

"This is . . . *nice*," Mikie said with awe and puzzlement.

"Who'd of thunk it?" I laughed.

Just then Paul Burman brushed by us. He and Mike had ignored each other the whole week. Burman, I think, still hated that Mikie had spent two weeks trying to make a basketball player out of him.

"Hey," Mike said, grabbing Burman's arm spontaneously. Burman turned and glared at him. I took a step back, waiting for the fight to come and blow up the whole deal, to make this slot a little more like the rest.

But silently Mikie led us over to the other easel, half hidden away in the corner. He pulled off the cloth and showed us his painting. It was of a basketball game. In the scene, a guard who looked something like Mike had just heaved an alley-oop pass to a nine-foot string bean who looked something like Burman, who was in the process of jamming it home.

They both burst out laughing. The string bean was totally naked, his privates flying every which way.

They didn't say anything more about it. But the tension was all gone. They'd settled it their own way.

I wasn't finished with it, though.

"This was very good for you, Mikie," I prodded. "It's kind of like, well, admitting you were *wrong* about something. This is good, this is good. Let's keep going with this—"

"Let's not," Mikie said, and tried to spin away from me.

I grabbed his arm and pulled him back. "Come on now, let's not lose our momentum. Say, 'I was *wrong* to try to force Paul to be a basketball star.'"

"That's not necessary," Paul said, laughing.

"No, no, no, Paul," I lectured. "Michael has a problem, and you are what they call an enabler. You must stop making it easier for him. He needs to do this."

"Shut up, El," Mikie said, this time breaking cleanly away.

"Okay, Mike," I called. "We'll try again later. Meanwhile, try to keep expressing yourself through your art. And practice when nobody's listening: 'I was *wrong*. I made a *mistake*. I don't know *everything*. . . .'" I was enjoying myself thoroughly, though nobody was listening anymore. I stopped only when the exhibit resumed.

Brother Fox pulled back the cover on the table to expose Eugene's crude clay model of hands. Gigantic hands like his, sprouting up out of a flat base, turned upward with fingers spread, like you would do if you were examining your own hands for whatever reason. They were set in front of a chair so that we could all take turns sitting in position, trying on Eugene's massive mitts.

"Oh my god," Oskar said as he got his perspective on owning hands like those. "Gene, man, how do you scratch your balls without ripping them right off?"

Eugene cuffed him but clearly liked the attention. We were still laughing when we shifted down to the glass guy's orange cut-glass sunburst. It was beautiful like an explosion, and dangerous like one, as he'd spent hours and hours snapping and cracking the tiny glass rays around the edges so that they were so jagged and edgy that nobody but him could touch it without getting their hands sliced up into angel hair.

"I got a artwork for you boys!" the first deep yell came from outside.

"Yo, Mary, wanna see a sculpture?" the second one called.

"Oh, not this," Brother Percy sighed.

Eggs smashed rapid fire, like fat raindrops, on all the windows, all around the building. Then there were more laughs.

"Ignore it. It will blow over," Brother Mattus said. "Let's move on."

"Let's," Brother Percy said.

I looked around to see what the other guys felt, the guys who, unlike the Arts Brothers, had not seen it all before. Their bodies had all sort of shrunk, shriveled, as if they were hoping to suck into new turtle shells till it, please god, blew over. Except Oskar who, that's right, *had* seen this once before during his first freshman tour. He had his face pressed to the window, staring out numbly at them.

"We're comin', boys, whatchu gonna do?" the voice, Obie's voice, called. Then the voices started moving. Like hyenas, they screeched and circled the building, each one getting louder, pushing the others crazier, out of control.

"Somebody'll stop it," I said, trying to fool myself calm. The library was the most remote building in the compound, other than the unused seminarians' quarters, but still, wouldn't this be seen and heard across the campus? "These guys'll be caught."

Mikie looked at me stupid. "El, I've only been here a few days, but even *I* know better than that. The only people who are bothered by all this are in here."

"Maybe *we* should catch 'em," Eugene growled. He was pacing, his great big head and hands purple.

"Whoa, how 'bout another brownie, Eugene?" I asked. He ignored me.

"It'll pass. It always does," Brother Crudelle said nervously. He hurried to turn over the tape, which had snapped to a stop.

"Must be twenty or thirty of them this year," Oskar said from the window. The words were hardly out of his mouth before he added, "Shit," and hit the floor.

Crash, and *conk*, it shattered the window and bounced off the top of his head. It was a baseball.

"That's *it*!" Eugene screamed, and beat it for the door.

"Yaaa," Lennox yelled, and followed. Then Burman. Then Mikie. Then all the meek and feeble artsies, most moaning, "Oh my god," or hyperventilating words, like "Shit, shit, shit, shit."

"We're all gonna die," I added, as I found myself outside.

"No we're not," Oskar said, wearing the baseball lump on his forehead like a miner's beacon.

The whole pack of them—O's, sub-O's, and O wanna-bes—were well on their way by the time we got out there. They were running back up the hill, with a couple of our guys fanned out in a halfhearted chase. Except for Eugene. Eugene powered like a freight train, caught up to the last one, and felled him like a lion grabbing a zebra. As he finished the tackle hard and pushed the guy's face into the turf, I ran up to see. Everybody else had stopped chasing, but none of the tough guys came back to help this one.

Eugene had his massive fist raised and was about to drop it when the pleading started. "I'm sorry, I'm sorry, I mean it, I'm sorry," Frank said.

I grabbed Eugene's fist with both hands. It was like holding a bumpy cantaloupe. "He kind of belongs to me," I said, embarrassed.

"You should think about picking your friends more carefully, Elvin," Eugene growled, giving Frankie's head a hard shove before getting off him and marching away.

"I'm sorry, El. I'm sorry," Frank said, his speech a little fuzzy. He was saying it now not because he didn't want to get smacked, but because he was *sorry*. "It wasn't my idea. I'll stop them myself if they try it again. I didn't even—"

Frank had looked past me toward where Mikie was coming to investigate. He wouldn't let Dad see him now, so he bolted, back up the hill.

Mikie and I watched the last of the retreat. All of them ran as easily uphill as if it was downhill. All of them athletic. All of them strong and fast and tough and brave. All of them The Chosen.

They were wearing sunglasses and ski hats, a couple with hoods. But it didn't really matter.

Mikie pulled up beside me. "Frankie almost bought it that time," he said grimly.

"Come on, come on," Brother Clarke said to each of us as we marched back in the door. "Drink? Drink, sure, there you go. Don't let it spoil a fine time."

"Ya," big Brother Mattus said, circulating among us

now, handing to each one a big stick. Some of us got broom handles, the janitor push-broom kind with the metal screw-in tip. Others got those old long-handled devices with the hook on the end for opening and closing tall windows. "Ya, we're not going to let them spoil *our* fine time, are we?" He took his own pole and smacked it loudly against the hardwood floor.

Once again I looked at the faces all around me, trying to feel what I was supposed to feel. I decided I was feeling the correct feeling because the uneasiness inside me was splashed across every other face as well. What were we going to do, hunt them down?

"Yessirree," Brother Fox announced, marching to the center of the room. "He who laughs last . . . Right?"

"Right!" the Brothers chimed together, while the students sat in chilled silence. Who were these Rambo guys all of a sudden?

Brother Percy let out a knowing low chuckle as he swept up the broken glass by the window. He was always doing that, acting as if he knew stuff. It bothered me sometimes. It bothered me now.

"What do they have at their party up there?" Brother Fox shouted. "Okay, so they have beer. Well we have . . ." He reached up and yanked a string that was like a light switch, unveiling—". . . a piñata."

The Art Brothers had gotten together to build it, and it was professional. Papier-mâché, bigger than life size. It had angel's wings, and an angelic expression looking

234

heavenward. And it had Arnold Schwarzenegger muscles, shoulder pads, a baseball cap on backward. With one hand it was leaning on a baseball bat, with the other it was grabbing its crotch.

It was a dead ringer for Brother Jackson.

There was a lot of energy let out in that room then. Probably more than that library had seen in a hundred years put together. You could get close to the Jackson piñata only if you were willing to risk getting your own dome cracked. A risk almost everyone was willing to take.

Me, I felt no need. With every hard whack across one of Jackson's vital parts, I felt a warm central surge—like swallowing a cocoa-soaked Chips Ahoy without having to chew it. So I watched.

"You liked the book," Brother Percy said, sneaking up beside me.

I looked at him suspiciously, then let myself smile. "Is that okay, just to sit and watch, to look at people and think? I mean, is that an okay way to be?"

"Does it feel okay?" he asked.

I turned to watch the piñata beating, got another little thrill from it. "It does. It feels okay."

"Then it probably is," he said.

Then Eugene did it—he ripped that Jackson right in half with a chop. Out of him fell art supplies—water-colors, tubes of acrylic paint, small sketch pads, brushes, bricks of modeling clay.

"Thank you, Brother Jackson, mother of art," Brother Fox called out.

"Wouldn't it kill him?" Brother Percy responded.

"Let's hope so," said Brother Clarke.

There was no wild scrambling like if there was candy in the piñata. Everybody could pretty much tell what belonged to him. Brother Percy went to the pile and dug a couple of things out—a pocket-size notebook, and one of those Space Pens the astronauts took to the moon that you can write with upside down or under water. I figured it was like one of those general all-purpose presents that you keep under the Christmas tree for unexpected guests, say, like candy or a black scarf, that could work for anyone. But he gave them to *me*.

"And you can keep *Winesburg*," he said. "It's not really the library's. I planted it."

I walked back to Mikie's Cluster with him when it was all over.

"That was almost as good as a party *with* girls." He laughed.

I shook my head at it all. "Weird, isn't it? I told you they were weird. I don't know, Mike, I don't know what my slot is, or what it's going to be, or if I'm ever going to find a slot. But I figure I could hang out with these guys while I'm waiting."

He grinned as I left him at his door. "I bet you could," he said.

It was automatic when I woke up. I knew it was my last time and I wanted that run through the woods. My eyes were not even all the way open when I pulled my running stuff on.

I checked before I left, and Frankie was not home yet. His bed was still empty.

Then I turned to go out and there he was in the doorway. He leaned on the doorframe because he couldn't stand too well. His pressed shirt was gone, his pleated shorts were gone. All he was wearing were his gray Calvin Klein boxer briefs he was always so proud to flash for everyone. He didn't move—he didn't speak. He had dusty dirt and scuff marks all over his arms, legs, and belly. His perfect pretty face was drained and shellacked with tears. He was crying. He wasn't making a sound, but it was pouring out of him.

There are some things a guy just should never have to see.

I was standing in the narrow corridor between the front door and the bathroom. Frankie waved at me, a brushing motion telling me to get out of the way. I stepped aside. Stumbling, knees buckling and then locking, he wobbled his way along, brushing past me. I didn't turn until he was by me. His back was covered with scratches.

I didn't say anything, but he rasped at me to just shut up anyway. Then, as he passed Thor's bed, he fell down, like sombody'd clubbed him.

I ran to him, started helping him up.

"Don't tell Mikie," Frankie sobbed. "Don't tell Mikie. Elvin, don't tell Mikie."

Thor sat up.

"No," Frankie said to him. "No, please. Just ignore us."

Thor started getting up. He looked sad. But he didn't look surprised.

"Please, Thor," I whispered.

He hesitated. "You can handle it?"

"What a question," I thought. No, I cannot.

"I can handle it," I said. "Go back to bed, Thor."

"If you can't, Elvin, I'm gonna have to get involved," he said. "I should help anyway . . ."

"No," Frankie said, more desperately now. His voice rose, so I covered his mouth with my hand.

"You want anybody else up for this?" I asked Frankie. He shook his head no.

I waved Thor off, and he settled back into his bed.

"Frankie's lucky," Thor said. "When it happened to Obie, he didn't have any good friends to take care of him."

I pulled Frankie's underwear off and shoved him into the shower.

"Don't tell Mikie," Frank pleaded. "Don't tell Mikie."

"I'll do better than that," I said. "I'm not going to tell *myself*." I tried to hold him up and get some soap on him at the same time. I had never tried to wash another person before in my life, so it was awkward. I tried at first not to

238

look at him as I did it, but I realized how stupid that was, so I just did it. I felt him trembling. Though it may have been me.

"I did it, El," he said when he finally had it together enough to stand and lather himself. I toweled myself off. "I'm made. They couldn't break me, and now I'm made. I'm king. I'm guaranteed. It's like in the Mafia. Once you're made, you're in for good. You're picked. I made it, El."

"You're a man, Franko," I said, as convincingly as I could.

"Ya, El. Only now I'm a man's man."

He tried to laugh at his own joke, but as he did, he almost passed out. I reached in and caught him. Got myself all soaked again.

"Don't tell Mikie," he said. "Elvin, I don't want you to tell Mikie."

I shut off the water, dried him, wrapped him in a towel, and wrestled his broken grown-man's body to his bed. He was out before he even got there.

I promised him anyway that I wouldn't tell.

"Come here, Elvin," Thor whispered then. "Maybe we should talk. You want to talk about it?"

"Can't," I said, holding a stiff-arm block in Thor's direction.

I hurried, hurried to the door, blasted out, ran my run.

When we got on the bus for the ride home, Frankie sat way in the back, and nobody took the seat next to him.

Funny how even when people don't know something, they really do know. Mikie and I sat together in front of him. All the way, Mikie was just as silent as me, just as silent as Frank.

I never did tell him. Even though it was the first important thing *ever* that I didn't tell him in my whole life. For once I wasn't going to dump it on him. This one was for me to carry, and I carried it myself.

After riding quiet with Mikie for a while, I got up and moved to the seat behind me, next to Frankie. He looked at me kind of grimly at first. Then a half Mona Lisa came across his pouty, pretty mouth before he looked away again out the window.

It was still quiet, but it was better.

I took out my new pen and my little pad.

"Another letter, Elvin?" Mikie said, leaning over the back of his seat. "You're going to be there in another hour and a half, for god's sake."

"I know it," I said. "It's just, I guess I've developed a habit here."

Dear Mom,

I don't suppose you knew, exactly, when you sent me, how it would happen, but I guess it happened. I've seen the world in three weeks.

I'm not an athlete, Mom. Hope you're not disappointed.

And I don't think I'm going to be a priest, though we haven't ruled that out.

240

It will be really refreshing to be rejected by a girl again. I can't wait.

I left home with two friends, and I'm returning with two (not counting you). But when you see us, don't try to talk to us too much right away, because we probably won't want to. Frankie's changed, a lot. And I've changed, although I couldn't really tell you how, since I don't think I actually did anything here.

And even though I fought it the whole way, I woke up this morning and realized that all three of us have been slotted. On the outside it looks like this: Mikie fits everywhere; Frankie is King; and I'm a refugee.

But on the inside, it goes like this: Mikie is still One; Frankie is still One-A; and I'm still whatever it is I am.

They can't touch that.

See you in an hour.

Love,
El